# A FAMILIAR FEELING

BY

## MARGARET BARKER

CW00376285

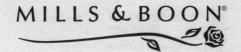

MILLS & BOON®

*First published in Great Britain 1999*
*Harlequin Mills & Boon Limited,*
*Eton House, 18-24 Paradise Road, Richmond, Surrey TW9 1SR*

© Margaret Barker 1999

ISBN 0 263 81834 9

*Set in Times Roman 10½ on 12 pt.*
*03-9911-51575-D*

*Printed and bound in Spain*
*by Litografia Rosés S.A., Barcelona*

# CHAPTER ONE

'IT REALLY is you, isn't it? *C'est toi*, Caroline.'

Caroline stared at her new boss. What exactly did he mean? She'd been speaking in her best French, slightly in awe of him, certainly unprepared for the fact that he was using the familiar *tu* instead of the appropriate *vous* when he addressed her. He surprised her even further when he announced,

'*C'est mois, Pierre!*'

She stared at the handsome stranger whom she'd never seen before in her life!

'Dr Chanel,' she began tentatively, 'I think you're mistaken. I—'

'On, come on, now, Caroline. Surely you haven't forgotten the time I brought you back from the hay fields on the top of the waggon? Your grandmother was furious with me and—'

'Pierre! *Mais, bien sûr!*'

Suddenly the mists of time had evaporated and she was back in her childhood days, laughing and joking with the boy next door. Or so she'd thought of Pierre, even though she'd only met him at holiday times when she'd stayed with her grandmother and he'd been helping out on his uncle's farm. She screwed up her eyes so that she could superimpose the teenage features on the adult face above her—very much above her!

Yes, she remembered the distinctive hazel eyes, the prominent nose, the wide mouth with crinkly, kindly creases at the side, always ready to erupt into a smile or a laugh.

'So, you really didn't know it was my Clinique when you applied for the job?' he asked incredulously.

'I haven't seen you since I was about nine. I never knew your surname and I certainly didn't know you were a doctor. Wait a minute, yes! I remember you said you were going to go to medical school. That was why you didn't come back in the summer any more, I suppose.'

Completely unbidden, the familiar ache returned to the pit of her stomach as she remembered that first summer without Pierre. She'd been all alone with her grandmother; nobody around to liven up the long days. Even though Pierre had been nine years older than she, he'd been generous with his time, letting her help him feed the hens and the cows, supplying her with a wooden rake so that she could pull the dried grass into neat rows—not so neat in her own case!

She looked around her at the familiar, yet now unfamiliar surroundings of the Clinique de la Tour. This reception area had been her grandmother's sitting room. The tall ceiling still had the ornate alabaster carvings round the edge, which she'd always thought was in keeping with how a château should look.

'It's still very grand, isn't it?' she said. 'You know, in my grandmother's day, when it was called Château de la Tour, I used to love telling my schoolfriends in England that I was going to stay in a real castle—especially when I only lived in a tiny flat in the London suburbs with my mother!'

'Your mother never came with you, did she?'

She steeled herself to cope with the emotional pain. 'She was never very strong. The idea was to give her a break from looking after me. When they diagnosed her leukaemia…'

'I'm so sorry. I didn't know. Is she…?'

Caroline cleared her throat. 'She lived longer than we expected. She died five years ago.'

Five years years ago when Caroline had decided to go for her dream and buy Château de la Tour back with the money her grandmother had left in trust for her until she was twenty-five. But she'd been pipped at the post by an unknown buyer.

'When did you buy Clinique la Tour, Pierre?' she asked casually.

'When it first came on the market, five years ago. Your grandmother had sold it to the local doctor when she had to go into hospital—just before she died, I believe—and he sold it when he retired. There were lots of people interested in the property so I had to settle the deal quickly. It's such a beautiful old building.'

'Yes, I've always loved it.'

She allowed her eyes to wander over to the idyllic scene outside the windows—rolling hills as far as the eye could see, tall trees shading the garden, warm brown cows browsing in the meadow beyond the stone wall. Her grandmother had wanted her to have all this. She'd had to sell the château to pay for her expensive nursing-home treatment, but she'd told Caroline that if there was any money left when she died she hoped it would be enough to buy it back.

As it happened, she hadn't lived very long after leaving the château and her legacy had increased over the years so that it would have been perfectly possible…

'You look as if you're miles away, Caroline! You must be tired after your journey. I'll get one of the nurses to take you up to your room. Have a rest and then we'll talk later. I've got to go and see a patient now.'

She followed the trim, white-cotton-dressed nurse out of the reception area into what should have been the familiar entrance hall. But everything had been changed out of recognition! She paused by the open door of the kitchen, half expecting to see her grandmother mixing one of her delicious gateaux. Instead, she saw that the kitchen was now a waiting room. The notices on the three closed doors proclaimed that they were consulting rooms. One of these would soon be hers. A shiver of apprehension threatened to undermine her usual self-confidence. Would it be the old television room or the music room where she'd practised all those endless scales for her piano exams?

'Dr Bennett?'

She turned away quickly, remembering the nurse who was waiting for her on the stairs.

'Sorry to keep you waiting, Nurse. I haven't been back to this house since I was a child. There's so much to see and—'

'Did you live here, Doctor?'

'On and off. I was very happy here. It was my only real home.'

They had reached the first floor. Caroline didn't know why she was confiding in this young, blonde-haired nurse, apart from the fact that she had a friendly smile and a sympathetic manner.

'Where did you live when you weren't here?'

'In London.'

'You don't sound English.'

Caroline smiled. 'My father is English, my mother was French, so I suppose I'm half and half.' She looked around her at the array of unfamiliar doors leading from the landing. 'What are the rooms on this floor?'

The young nurse smiled, making Caroline feel more at home—if that were possible in the place which had been completely taken over and out of her hands!

'This is where we house our inpatients. There are more rooms in the new annexe in the garden but most patients prefer to have a room in the main part of the château if they can.'

'My room used to be through there,' Caroline said. 'Facing south-east. I used to lie in bed and watch the sun rise and listen to the cows mooing at the farm as they were milked.'

She took a deep breath as she told herself she must stop all this nostalgia stuff! She was here to do a job of work, and dreaming about the past wasn't going to help her to be efficient.

'Dr Chanel has given you a room on the top floor where we have our staff quarters.'

Caroline turned the corner in the stairs, pleased to see that the ancient, rather unsafe and rickety banister had been replaced by a sturdy oak handrail.

'Voila!' The young nurse threw open one of the doors. 'This is your room, Doctor. You have a small shower room en suite…'

Caroline followed her across the room to inspect the tiny cabinet de toilette, glad that she was small enough to squeeze in. It certainly wouldn't be big enough for a larger person! The tiny porthole window above the minuscule handbasin looked out over the garden. Standing on tiptoe, she could see Pierre walking in the garden in earnest conversation with a middle-aged woman dressed in a woollen suit—a convalescent patient perhaps? There were other patients strolling round the garden in the late afternoon sunshine, some in dressing-gowns, others fully clothed.

She was longing to see the garden to see what changes

had been made. Would the bluebells she'd so loved still be in the small orchard at the end of the garden? Or would some efficient gardener have decided that wild flowers weren't in keeping with the chic image of the Clinique? First she'd better unpack and then—

'Do you need anything else, Doctor?'

She came out of her reverie with a start, having forgotten she wasn't alone. 'No, I'm fine. Thank you, Nurse.'

The young woman closed the door softly behind her. Caroline unlocked her case and opened the lid. She'd brought only lightweight clothing. It had been hot when she'd left Hong Kong. Pulling out the cream linen suit which she'd worn when David Howard, the director of the Hong Kong nursing home, had taken her out to dinner a couple of nights ago, she reflected that he'd been very understanding when she'd asked for a six-month break from her job.

She unwrapped the tissue paper around it, noting that it wasn't too creased to wear without ironing, thank goodness! Ironing wasn't her strong point. In her quarters in the Hong Kong nursing home she'd been blessed with a daily maid who'd dealt with laundry. Even in this smart-looking Clinique, Caroline doubted there would be domestic help for the staff.

Teaching her to wrap her clothes in tissue paper, that was one of the many things which had made her grateful to her grandmother. The very first time she'd arrived here in the château, at the age of five, with a suitcase full of creased clothes, stuffed in by her weary mother in wild disarray, her grandmother had shown her how to wrap everything in tissue paper.

Caroline crossed the small room in a couple of easy strides and opened the wardrobe. Six hangers waited to be occupied. That should be enough. It was a good thing she'd left behind the rest of the clothes she'd accumulated over five years of wonderful shopping in Hong Kong!

Returning to remove her cotton skirt and a couple of blouses, she reflected that David had certainly been very understanding in letting her leave her job for six months. Not many bosses would have been so understanding. She hushed the pang of guilt that threatened to nag her. It wasn't her fault if David was beginning to entertain unwelcome ideas about her. She'd always made it quite clear that she was only interested in a professional relationship with him.

And, to give him his due, her farewell dinner at the Furama restaurant, overlooking Hong Kong harbour, had been a very light-hearted occasion. He hadn't become sentimental or demanding. It was just that look in his eyes when she'd told him she wanted to return to her roots for a while, get rid of the restlessness that often overtook her and—

The phone was ringing. Where in the world was the wretched thing? She unearthed it, covered in a pile of tissue paper, from the bedside table.

'Âllo?'

'Caroline, it's Pierre. I wanted to catch you before you went off to sleep to say—'

'Oh, I'm not going to go to sleep till tonight.'

'Not too jet-lagged?'

She laughed. 'If I keep going for a few hours longer I'll get a good night's sleep and then I'll be fine in the morning. That's what I always do when I come home—I mean, back to Europe. I'd like to see something of the hospital while it's still daylight. I'll be down in ten minutes.'

'OK. I'll be on the first floor in room six with a patient.'

She showered and pulled on a cotton dress. As she ran

down the stairs to the first floor she reflected that it was warm for the beginning of May and, coupled with the fact that radiators still threw out their heat in most areas, she knew that the cold European temperatures she'd dreaded hadn't materialised.

Room six felt even hotter. She must speak to Pierre about bringing down the temperature in the château. But would he resent her intervention? It was, after all, his Clinique, not hers. She felt a pang of resentment that she should only be an employee in the château which should have been hers. If only…

She made a deliberate effort to stop that destructive train of thought as she looked at Pierre. He was standing by the bedside of a motionless patient. He turned and smiled as she entered the white, sterile-looking room. Flowers filled every corner and surface but the bed looked clinical enough. The tubes and attachments enveloping their patient pointed to the fact that here was a desperately ill patient. Caroline recognised the middle-aged woman in the woollen suit that she'd seen from the window sitting in the corner, reading a magazine.

Pierre introduced them. 'Mrs Smith, this is Dr Bennett. Mrs Smith is Katie's mother. Katie had an accident in England and she's been in a coma for six weeks. She was transferred here from hospital in London last week because the Smiths live in France.'

A very neat résumé, Caroline thought. Short, succinct and to the point, telling her—although perhaps not the patient's mother—that there was very little hope of Katie coming out of this coma. In effect, the high-tech hospital which had first cared for her had decided there was nothing more they could do and that the kindest thing would be to let nature take its course whilst she was near her family.

She'd seen cases like this before where brain scans had showed the patients to be in a permanent vegetative state.

Poor girl! Caroline approached the bed and put her hand on the cold, unresponsive forehead.

'Hello, Katie.'

'She can't hear you,' Mrs Smith said, putting down her magazine and coming over to stand beside Caroline. 'I've been with her night and day for the past six weeks and she's never shown a sign of life.'

Mrs Smith clenched her teeth and drew in her breath with a distraught hissing sound.

'At first I used to talk to her all the time, even sing— you know, her favourite nursery rhymes, even though she's twenty,' she said, looking around at the two doctors with an air of embarassment.

'But then I got so tired and so depressed and I could see it was useless. It was almost a relief when the doctors said we could take her home. We live in Montreuil. My husband is setting up a computer business there.'

Caroline put her hand on the older woman's shoulder. 'You must never give up hope. Keep talking to your daughter even though you think she can't hear you. The brain is a very complex organ.'

Pierre was mouthing something at her, probably wanting her to stop raising the poor woman's hopes. But Caroline was remembering a case in Hong Kong—a car-accident victim who'd survived against all odds. Since she'd worked on that case she had always been wary of making drastic diagnoses where the brain was concerned.

A nurse came in with a tray. Caroline watched as the nourishing fluid was poured into the tube that went into Katie's stomach. There was no reaction from their patient. She turned away to scan the charts at the end of the bed.

Katie Smith, age 20, severe brain damage following car crash. No visible signs of—

Pierre's hand on her arm made her look up from her reading. His eyes told her that it really was a hopeless case. She knew she shouldn't become emotionally involved with her patients but it was already too late. One of the disadvantages of being an emotional person was that it was very difficult to remain detached from suffering.

And all her medical training told her that this was what she must do where this case was concerned. She must use all the medical expertise she could but accept the outcome, without too much agonising over what should or should not have been done.

'You'll take some rest, won't you, Mrs Smith?' Pierre said. 'Go out in the garden again for some fresh air as often as you like. One of the nurses will sit with Katie.'

The weary mother turned distaught eyes on Pierre and assured him she would take care of herself.

Outside in the corridor Caroline turned to Pierre. 'We had a similar case in Hong Kong. All the high-tech methods had failed and the patient was declared brain dead— but he survived.'

Pierre put a hand under her arm, steering her towards the steps with determined fingers.

'Caroline, please! Keep your voice down.'

Immediately, she resented his tone of voice. He was speaking to her as if she were still a child.

'Pierre, in case you haven't noticed, I've grown up!'

He stood still on the landing at the top of the staircase and his handsome face lit up with a heart-rending smile.

'I had noticed! Believe me, it's very obvious.'

She could feel an embarassing flush spreading over her cheeks as she looked up at him. His hazel eyes were alive with amusement. He was enjoying her discomfiture. She felt he was being patronising and...and something else. Something that hadn't been there in those expressive eyes when she was a child.

How simple relationships were when you were a child! You were never on the look-out for tell-tale signs that told you to be on your guard. Pierre had been the big brother she'd never had. How could he look at her now as if he was admiring her as a woman? That wasn't what she wanted from him. She wanted their easygoing, uncompli- cated relationship to continue.

She tensed, but the look in his eyes had gone and he was serious again.

'I'm sorry, Caroline. You were making a valid point,' he said slowly.

'This patient of yours, is he fully recovered?'

She hesitated. Brian Wilson was far from recovered. 'It's early days. He's going to need full-time care, of course, but he's alive.'

'And how about the quality of his life?'

They were descending the staircase now, reaching the narrow part where it was difficult to walk two abreast with- out touching each other. She stepped behind him, watching the broad back, the longer than average hair that trailed over his collar in a careless ridge of dark waves.

'It will improve,' she said carefully, more in hope than relying on medical facts.

'I always think that quality of life is more important than quantity,' he said as he stepped off the bottom stair.

Turning round, he put both hands on the sides of her shoulders and looked down into her eyes with a meaning- ful expression.

'Nature will take its course with Katie when medical science can do no more,' he said quietly.

She remained silent and watched as he pulled himself

to his full height. 'How about some dinner? If you're not too tired, I'll take you out on the town.'

'Out on the town?'

He laughed at her incredulous tone. 'It's not only London and Paris that have bright lights, you know. You were too young to appreciate the finer points of this area when you were here before. Montreuil sur Mer is just a few kilometres down the road and there are some excellent restaurants.'

She realised she was hungry. She hadn't eaten much on the long flight from Hong Kong to London and had only managed a sandwich on the train in the Channel tunnel.

Looking up at Pierre, she smiled. 'Yes, I'd like that. Actually, I'm starving!'

'Good. I remember you never refused a *baguette de jambon* when it was offered to you in the fields. My uncle used to be amazed that such a small child could make large amounts of food disappear. I must say, even with your voracious appetite, you've stayed quite petite.'

Her answer came automatically. She'd got used to countering the remarks people made about her being small. 'Diamonds come in small packages.'

'I'm sorry, I meant it as a compliment. Half the women in the western world would kill for a figure like yours.'

She felt the unwelcome flush spreading over her cheeks again. 'No need to go over the top! Now you've roused my interest in food, how soon can we eat?'

'I've got a few things to organise first. Say in half an hour?'

'Fine!'

She ran up the stairs, wondering if he was still watching her. She felt unusually aware of the effect he was having on her. But when she turned the corner of the stairs and hazarded a glance downwards she breathed a sigh of relief to see that he'd gone.

What a jumble of emotions she was experiencing! Must be the jet lag getting to her and giving her an over-stimulated imagination.

In her room she changed into the cream linen suit. In the pocket she found the menu she'd picked up at the Furama restaurant only two evenings ago. She was certainly beginning to live it up! Dinner in two different continents in such a short time and with two different men.

Entirely different! David was of medium height, stockily built and fair-haired. Dark-haired Pierre seemed to be the tallest man she'd ever known and he certainly seemed much more athletic. Of course, David must be a few years older than Pierre. What was David now? Forty-five? Whereas Pierre, her teenage idol, was only—heaven above, he must be an astounding thirty-nine! Positively one foot in the proverbial… But he didn't look it. He was still handsome, debonair, dashing—all the things she admired in a man, so long as he kept his distance!

She leaned nearer to the tiny mirror over the washbasin as she applied her lipstick. Why was she comparing these two men? Both were good friends and colleagues. Nothing more, nothing less, and that was the way it would stay.

She found Pierre in Reception, talking to a tall young man with fair, wavy hair. He broke off and smiled at her.

'This is Dr Jean Cadet, who's going to be in charge tonight while I'm away. Dr Caroline Bennett is with us for a few months while Giselle is on maternity leave.'

Dr Cadet put out his hand. '*Enchanté!* Delighted to meet you, Dr Bennett.'

Caroline grasped the proffered hand and in a quick assessment decided that she liked the look of this effusive young man. The clean, starched, white coat over his grey suit gave him an efficient air.

'OK, we'll see you later, Jean. You can call me on the mobile if you need to.'

Jean Cadet smiled. 'Emergencies only, I think. Enjoy yourselves.'

'Of course.' Pierre put his hand under Caroline's elbow and steered her out through the door .

The sun was sinking rapidly over the farm buildings beyond the side wall of the garden as Pierre took her towards his sleek, silver-coloured car and opened the passenger door. She sank into the black leather-cushioned seat.

'Mmm, very smart, Pierre! Positively opulent.'

He laughed as he slotted the key into the ignition. 'An improvement on the hay waggon, I think.'

'I'll say! Where are you taking me?'

'Somewhere extremely posh!'

She laughed as she heard him speaking English for once. 'Your accent hasn't improved!'

'Well, thank you very much!' He gave a mock frown as he negotiated the difficult turn out into the road. 'Just because you're totally bilingual it doesn't allow you to make fun of we lesser mortals. I'll have you know I've been taking lessons to improve my English so that I can talk to my English patients.'

'Very commendable. Don't get me wrong, Pierre, I think your French accent is very charming.'

'At last, a compliment! So you think I'm very charming, do you?'

'I said your accent was very charming.'

She looked out of the window, feeling unsure of the direction of the conversation again. Coming to terms with this sophisticated, mature Frenchman who had once thrown her over his shoulder and hoisted her on to a hay waggon, it was proving difficult.

Should she continue in the same bantering, easy, friendly manner, or should she put up the invisible barrier she usually erected when dealing with a possible threat to her independence?

But this is Pierre, your surrogate big brother, she reasoned. He's got to be different to all the rest—hasn't he? She looked out of the window at the side road which led to the village.

'Grand-mère used to send me down to the *boulangerie* for the baguettes and croissants when I was nine. I used to feel very grown up.'

'It wouldn't be safe now. Far too much traffic on these narrow country lanes. I blame it on the English invasion.'

'Oh, very funny.' Knowing Pierre as she did, she recognised that his tongue was firmly in his cheek! 'Are there many English people in the area?'

'Loads of them. They've bought up all the old ruins that the French wouldn't touch with a bargepole and converted them into wee little second homes.'

'Hey, steady on! I'm not sure I approve of your tone, Dr Chanel.'

He slammed on the brakes to avoid a cat that shot across the road and disappeared into a cottage garden. Turning to look at her before putting his foot back on the accelerator, he smiled.

'As you English say, I am winding you up. We all love the English really. And quite a number of new businesses are being created by the people who settle here, which is good for the economy. Mrs Smith's husband, for example, already employs twenty people in Montreuil in his computer business.'

'So it looks as if he'll be able to afford your fees, Doctor.'

'You're fishing, aren't you?' For an instant he took his eyes off the road and glanced sideways, a wry smile on his full lips.

She grinned. 'Well, I was wondering about how you financed the château—sorry, the Clinique.'

'It's quite simple. It's a private *clinique* but the fees are moderate and most of my patients are covered by some kind of insurance. I'm not interested in making money, only in caring for my patients. And I do take state health system patients if they're referred to me by another doctor.'

'But you will always own Château de la Tour, even after you retire?'

'*Exactement!* It will always be mine.'

She looked out of the window at the river winding through the valley. 'You're very lucky,' she said quietly.

'I know!'

She drew in her breath. He still hadn't picked up on the fact that she was annoyed. No—more than annoyed, she was furious with him for stealing her château. She could hear her grandmother's voice in her mind, telling her to buy back the château if it was at all possible.

The day before Grand-mère had gone into hospital for the last time she'd called Caroline into her sitting room and apologised for having sold the château. She'd explained that it had been the only way she could raise the money for her medical treatment.

'But I'm putting all the money in your name. Whatever is left is yours when you are twenty-five,' she'd said.

Caroline gave a sigh as she remembered the thin, quavery voice.

'Hey, cheer up! What's your problem?'

She sat up straight and clenched her hands together. 'Sorry…I was just remembering my grandmother, what a wonderful woman she was. So wise.'

They were coming to the outskirts of Montreuil, going over the level crossing and driving up the winding road towards the mediaeval stone walls. Pierre slowed to allow a descending car to negotiate the arched entrance, before driving carefully through into the old city.

'I must admit she scared me a bit when I used to deliver you back to the château, Caroline, but I suppose she had to be tough with no man about the place. Your grandfather must have died earlier, I presume.'

'Hah! Grand-mère always wished she had been a widow, she told me. Grand-père deserted her for a younger woman and spirited away most of her money. She'd inherited the château and a large legacy from her father. She used to say that she was convinced that Grand-papa had only married her for her money.'

'How sad! I can't imagine anything so awful.'

'I can. It happened to my mother as well. My father— Sorry, Pierre. You don't want to hear my life history.'

'I do, I do!'

'But not while you're parking the car!' She smiled. 'Let's change the subject before I get carried away with the story of my wicked father and grandfather. It's all in the past now.'

All in the past. Only the legacy of what had been instilled into her by her mother and grandmother lived on. Keep your independence.

She looked around her at the smart hotel entrance near the car. Her hand reached to open the car door but Pierre was hurrying round to open it for her.

'What a gentleman!' She smiled up at him as she climbed out, thinking that it was nice to accept the old-fashioned courtesies. Theoretically, she ought to refuse to go along with that sort of thing if she meant to maintain her independence.

But it felt so sort of...feminine to be cherished and spoiled occasionally. And there was a certain kind of man who seemed to enjoy observing these small courtesies.

Had her father and her grandfather been like this when they'd taken out her mother and her grandmother in the early days? But that had been completely different. Her situation was one of colleague and old friend, and this relationship was firmly fixed in the platonic—wasn't it?

They were walking through a garden towards the entrance to the hotel. Small lights hidden in the bushes and behind the exotic plants gave the twilit garden an aura of splendour. Pierre put a hand on the small of her back and ushered her through the open door. She found the touch of his fingers strangely comforting.

Glancing sideways, she found herself unexpectedly proud to be accompanied by such a personable man. His tall stature and impressively confident bearing made him the sort of man that made people take a second glance. A waiter was guiding them towards a table set in a secluded alcove, overlooking the garden. Looking out, she saw that the sun had completely set, leaving only a rosy glow in the darkening sky.

Pierre's fingers closed over hers as he leaned across the white tablecloth. 'Welcome home, Caroline!'

His fingers clasped hers for a fraction of a second but she found it extremely disconcerting. It was merely a friendly gesture, she knew that for sure. But it unnerved her. This was meant to be a dinner between colleague and old friend, not an occasion to churn up the sort of unwelcome emotions that were fluttering around inside her.

He was raising his glass towards her now. She lifted hers and sipped the cold white wine.

'You always told me that this area was where you felt most at home,' he said quickly. 'Though perhaps you've changed your ideas. Maybe you prefer Hong Kong now.'

'No, I feel at home here,' she said, as she allowed her eyes to meet his across the table.

There was a buzzing sound as Pierre's mobile made its unwelcome presence heard. He swore quietly as he extricated it from his pocket and whispered into the receiver.

'What the hell does she want that can't wait?' Caroline heard him say.

The conversation was short and succinct, culminating in Pierre's final click before stuffing the offending object back in his pocket.

He took a gulp of wine, before looking across at Caroline. 'Trust Monique to interrupt my off-duty time!'

'Who's Monique?'

'My wife.'

# CHAPTER TWO

'YOUR wife?'

Caroline realised that she'd raised her voice in concern, but couldn't think why she should feel so upset. It was perfectly natural for Pierre to have a wife, wasn't it? It was just that she hadn't actually considered his marital situation. She'd imagined that nothing had changed since she'd last seen him and that—

'My ex-wife,' he said, putting great stress on the fact that she was ex.

For some unknown reason, she felt her spirits lifting. 'So you were married?' she said, regretting the inane remark as soon as she'd made it.

He grinned. 'Obviously! Now I suppose you'll want the full story.'

'No, I won't!' she lied, toying with the starched napkin which the waiter had placed on her lap. 'Not unless you want to tell me,' she added mock-coyly, looking up at him from under her eyelashes with the sort of expression she'd noticed in women who tried to manipulate men.

He leaned forward, a wry, lopsided smile highlighting the creases at the side of his full lips. His eyes held an intense expression.

'I think we'd better order first. It's a long, sad story— well, not sad any more because I'm free! And that's the way I intend to stay. I know it's a cliché but I really mean it when I say never again!'

She picked up the menu and stared, unseeing, at the first

page. 'But if you're divorced, why does—er, Monique still contact you?'

'Because she owns half the château and she's always checking up on her investment.'

She stared at him across the table, butterflies seeming to flap in her stomach. The fact that this woman, whom she already disliked, even without meeting her—after all, anybody who got a divorce from Pierre couldn't be worth knowing… The fact that this woman owned half her château was unthinkable!

'Pierre, I…'

He put his hand across the table and pointed to the starters on the menu. 'I thought you were hungry. Order something, Caroline.'

And without thinking, just as she had done when she was a child, she obeyed. When he'd told her not to go into the field with the nettles and she'd disobeyed him and got stung, she'd decided that Pierre had known best. Only halfway down the page of starters did she realise that she'd better recondition herself if she was going to survive as an adult woman with this complex character who'd had a whole lifetime of experiences since they'd last met.

She ordered *confit de canard*, a smooth-textured conserve of duck which seemed to melt in her mouth.

Pierre smiled at her as he wiped a napkin over his mouth and prepared to swallow another oyster.

'These are delicious! Want to try one?'

She leaned across the table and accepted the oyster that he'd loosened from its shell. It tasted of the sea, reminding her of the coastline not too far away, where she'd spent many happy hours digging in the sand while her grandmother had snoozed in the sunshine.

'I love oysters,' she told him, 'but I couldn't eat a dozen, like you.'

He laughed. 'Practice is all it takes. I can see it's a good thing you came back to France. This is the only country in the world where we take our cuisine seriously.'

'Oh, come on!' Caroline gave him a wry smile, realising once again that he was winding her up and she'd risen to the bait. Modifying her tone, she embarked on a list of the wonderful restaurants in Hong Kong and the delicacies she'd eaten there.

'Ah, but Hong Kong is the centre of international cuisine so you must have been spoiled for choice.' He paused and the expression in his eyes became more intense. 'What made you decide to work in Hong Kong?'

She put the final morsel of the *confit* in her mouth and chewed carefully, enjoying the taste of some unknown herb she couldn't yet identify. Pierre was right—should she spend more time back in France! He was still waiting for his answer. What should she say? Give him the shortened version?

'How long have you got?' she asked quietly.

He placed his napkin on the table and swished the tips of his fingers in the finger bowl. 'I'm not going anywhere. How about all night?'

He broke off and she knew he'd seen the flush that had risen to her cheeks. With some alarm, she saw a rakish grin spreading across his lips.

He corrected himself. 'I meant all evening, of course.'

'Well, I'll give you the shortened version,' she hurried on, before he could embarrass her further. 'I have two stepsisters and a stepmother living out there. My father invited me to join them for a holiday when I was about sixteen and—'

'But you said your mother only died five years ago. So your father must have—'

'That's right. Dad left us when I was very small, and

after the divorce came through he married a rich widow in Hong Kong who has two daughters older than me. They lived a rich lifestyle all through the years when Mum and I were struggling to get by and—'

'You sound bitter.'

She took a deep breath. 'I thought I was over it but it still rankles when I remember how hard it was for Mum. I was OK because children accept life as it comes so long as they're loved. And Mum loved me—and so did Grand-mère.'

The waiter was serving her with roast chicken so she stopped talking until he'd gone away.

'Go on, tell me some more.' Pierre was carving a portion of his steak and didn't look up.

'Dad didn't contact us and didn't reply when our solicitors tried to get maintenance money from him. Mum should have persevered, I suppose, but she was too ill to care most of the time and the solicitors were expensive. Then, out of the blue, when I was sixteen I got this invitation from Dad to go out to Hong Kong for a holiday.'

She speared a couple of slender *frites* and popped them in her mouth. Pierre was watching her, waiting for her to continue.

'And did you forgive your father?'

She shrugged. 'You mean, did I go out to see him with the family he'd cared for instead of Mum and me?' She paused as she remembered the cocktail of emotions she'd gone through at the time. Coupled with the changes taking place in her teenage years, it had been a difficult decision to make.

'Mum persuaded me to go out to Hong Kong. I think she was curious to know what kind of a life Dad was leading. It was certainly an eye-opener. I'd never known such luxury! Wonderful house on the Peak, swimming pool, servants and a wife who doted on him. Suzanne and Charlotte, my stepsisters, were more sceptical. They told me recently that they'd always suspected what he was up to but didn't want to disillusion their mother.'

She took a sip of her wine as the memories flooded back.

'And what was your father up to?'

'He was investing his wife's money in various hare-brained schemes, over-extending their finances and generally making a mess of things. When the crash came—as it inevitably did—he took off again and left his wife and stepdaughters to sort out the muddle.'

'When was this?'

She pulled a wry face. 'Ah, this is why I had to explain the situation. It was only a couple of years ago.'

'So you were actually out there at the time?'

She nodded. 'I certainly was! It was Suzanne and Charlotte who'd put the idea of me working in Hong Kong into my head. We'd written to each other after I'd first gone out there, and when Mum died, which was the same year that I qualified as a doctor incidentally, I—'

He reached across and patted her hand. 'That must have been a tough time for you.'

She drew in her breath as she felt the pricking at the back of her eyelids. 'Yes, it was—that was why I was pleased to hear from my stepsisters, who were urging me to go out to Hong Kong and work in a nearby nursing home. I had, originally, meant to return to France but—' She paused, wondering how to explain that Pierre had shattered her dream.

He was looking puzzled by her silence. 'So why didn't you?'

She took a deep breath. 'I knew that Dr Ribaud was

retiring and that Château de la Tour—sorry, Clinique de
la Tour—was on the market. I wanted to buy it. But—'

'But someone else got there first,' he said slowly.
'Caroline, I'm sorry, I had no idea.'

'Of course you didn't,' she said quickly. 'Anyway, if
I'd bought it I wouldn't have had the five interesting years
in Hong Kong. It's a great place, you know.'

She was chattering in her bright impersonal way, the
sort of tone she used with people she didn't know very
well.

'And you don't mind?'

'Mind? Why should I mind?' She met his gaze across
the table, swallowing her pride and determined not to let
him know that he'd snatched away her dream.

'So why did you come back to Château de la Tour?'

'I read the advert for a maternity leave doctor at Château
de la Tour in the UK medical journal we always get in
Hong Kong. I needed a break and I thought it would be
nice to spend some time in Europe. A temporary post is a
good idea. And I'll be able to go back refreshed and—'

'Caroline…you do mind, don't you? I understand you
better than you imagine.'

'Do you?'

'I know how much you loved the château when you
were a child and—'

'Let's talk about you for a change. It's your turn to bare
your soul. What about this wife of yours—sorry, ex-wife?'

He seemed uncharacteristically flustered. 'I'll get around
to her in a minute. One last question worries me. How on
earth did your mother come to be married to a man who
deserted her like that?'

She gave him a wry smile. 'Quite simple. She told me
she fell in love with him, and he always was a charmer—
sorry, *is* a charmer. He's charming his fourth wife in

America at the moment, although I don't know how long that will last—till the money runs out, I suppose.'

'Hang on! Did you say *fourth* wife?'

She put her fork down on the plate and leaned back against the cushioned surface of the elaborately carved chair.

'My mother was wife number two. She'd come to England from France to be an au pair in a family in London. My father's first family, that is.'

She watched Pierre's eyes widen with disbelief. 'Yes, I know it sounds far-fetched but it's all true. My father started making a pass at the young eighteen-year-old and she found him difficult to resist. He took her to Paris for a weekend and on the way back they stopped off at Château de la Tour. Grand-mère told me she disapproved of the whole affair but my father didn't let that put him off. When he saw the château, he decided my mother must be loaded. When she told him she was pregnant—with me, of course—he had no problem leaving his wife and family.'

'*Dessert, mademoiselle? Il y a…*'

Caroline told the waiter she wouldn't have dessert. 'Just coffee, please.'

'And how old were you when your father left you?' Pierre asked when the waiter was out of earshot.

She frowned as she tried to remember the day it had dawned on her that her father really wasn't coming back. 'Two or three. He was always travelling so it was difficult to realise whether he lived with us or not. When he'd managed to charm the woman who was to become wife number three in Hong Kong he left Mum and me. My grandmother had already announced that my mother had been cut out of her will in favour of me and I think he couldn't wait that long to get his hands on my money.'

'Your grandmother must have been furious that the same thing had happened to her daughter as—'

'Oh, she was very philosophical about it. Just told me to make sure it never happened to me. And it won't.'

'You sound very sure of yourself. What if you fell in love with a real charmer and he turned out to be a philanderer?'

'Oh, I'd have checked him out first.'

'Is this before or after you fall in love?'

'Oh, Pierre! Now you're making fun of me again.'

He spread his hands wide on the tablecloth, palms downwards. 'I swear I'm not! I just get the impression you're not very... How shall I put it? Very experienced where men are concerned. You've only got your father and grandfather as role models. What about your own love life?'

'Now you really are fishing! And I'm not going to answer one more question until you tell me about Monique.'

He took a final sip of coffee and replaced his cup in the saucer. 'I'm going to call for the bill and take you out for a stroll round the town. We both need some fresh air. And I'm not going to tell you about Monique tonight. You'll meet her soon enough, worse luck!'

'You mean she's here...here in Montreuil?'

He was trying to attract the waiter's attention. 'She phoned Jean Cadet at the hospital to say she was back at her cottage in the village. She's planning to visit the Clinique tomorrow.'

Pierre signed his name on the bill, before standing up and holding the back of her chair. 'Let's go!'

Walking round the town square, she breathed deeply to steady her nerves. The prospect of meeting Pierre's wife— the woman who owned half her château—wasn't a pleasant one.

They paused to admire the fountains in the middle of the square. The lights shone up at the cascade of iridescent water. Such a charming town! She was beginning to feel she was home at last. If only she could ignore the changes that she didn't like at the château. Changes like the fact that Pierre was still involved with his ex-wife. For some unknown reason she wanted him to be as free as she was.

He put an arm across her shoulders. 'You're shivering. It's too cold to be outside without a warm jacket. Here, take mine.'

And before she could protest, he'd draped his smooth, expensive woollen cloth jacket over her shoulders. It was still warm from his body. Mmm. She snuggled against the warm silk lining, luxuriating in the fresh scent of his aftershave.

Suddenly, she caught sight of him watching her with an amused expression. What was she doing, behaving like a starry-eyed teenager with a crush on an older man? She hadn't got a crush on Pierre, but he certainly roused sensual feelings inside her that she'd rather not dwell on! Looking at him now in the light surrounding the fountains, with the bright full moon up above, she could understand how people could fall in love.

It had never happened to her because she'd always kept a tight rein on her emotions. She'd had a few boyfriends but she'd never been tempted to surrender her heart, as it was described in the romantic fiction she sometimes indulged in. No, nothing like the emotions witnessed in the great classics had ever stirred her.

Until now! She held herself rigid as she realised she was fantasising about Pierre. It was purely an extension of the warmth she'd felt for him as a child, she told herself quickly. And the jet lag wasn't helping her think clearly either.

'I need to get some sleep,' she said quickly. 'If I'm to be any use to you tomorrow, we'd better call it a day.'

He pulled the jacket round in front of her and fastened the buttons. She remained stock-still, actually enjoying the feel of his fingers over the layers of clothing covering her breasts. Wanton, that was what she was being at the moment! She lifted her head and smiled.

'Thanks. Now, if you could just carry me back to the car I'll— No, I didn't mean it, Pierre. Put me down!' she shrieked, appalled at what she'd suggested.

He was laughing as he carried her out of the square, down a side street and back to the car. An old woman, putting her tabby-coloured cat out into the street, -called out, *'Ah! Les jeunes!'*

Caroline giggled. 'She thinks we're young.'

Pierre laughed. 'Well, I feel young tonight, don't you?'

'Maybe we're reverting to our childhood.'

'Doesn't do any harm now and again to let your hair down. Talking of which, when did you have your long hair cut off?'

He opened the passenger door, waiting until she was safely ensconced before going around to his side.

'About a year ago,' she said, suddenly feeling shy about discussing her appearance with Pierre. He'd never seemed to notice what she'd looked like in those early days. 'I fancied a change and a short hairstyle seemed sort of…' She broke off, searching for the right word.

'Chic,' he supplied, switching on the engine and manoeuvring the car out of the narrow space.

'I suppose so,' she admitted. 'But it's also very practical.'

'You can always grow it again,' he said quietly.

She drew in her breath but didn't reply. This concern about the way she looked was out of character with the

Pierre she'd known as a child and she didn't know how to handle it.

The bright full moon came from behind a cloud as they drove through the open wrought-iron gates of Clinique de la Tour. She could see the impressive round crenellated tower room at the top of the building, looking down on the tall trees which stood like sentries on either side of the drive, guarding the château. She felt very much at home even though there had been so many changes since she was last here.

She found herself wondering if Pierre would invite her to have a drink with him. She hoped so! Somehow, her jet lag seemed to have evaporated and she was wide awake.

As they went into the main reception area, Dr Jean Cadet looked up from the medical reports he was checking and smiled.

'Everything quiet, Jean?' Pierre asked.

'Mrs Smith rang down a couple of minutes ago. She'd like you to go up and see her before she sleeps. She thinks Katie moved one of her fingers.'

Pierre nodded. 'Did you check it out?'

Jean shook his head. 'I think it's wishful thinking and, anyway, she wants to see you about it.'

'Shall I come with you?' Caroline asked.

Pierre looked down at her, an enigmatic expression in his hazel eyes. 'It's time you were asleep. And you might start raising Mrs Smith's hopes too high.'

'I should be totally professional,' she countered, starting to walk away towards the stairs. 'See you in the morning.'

'Goodnight, Caroline.'

She was very much aware that he was watching her as she mounted the stairs. At the corner, she turned and looked down. He was smiling. She had the distinct impression that there was admiration in his eyes…or was she imagining it because that's what she was hoping for?

Hurriedly, she turned the corner, putting the treacherous thoughts from her head.

The sun was streaming in through Caroline's window when she awoke. She always slept with the curtains wide open so that she could see the moon—whenever there was one—and the stars, which had been particularly evident when she'd been living in Hong Kong. There was something about the clear skies in the Far East which made the stars look particularly beautiful.

Lying back against her pillows now, she remembered all the times she'd lain awake, watching the sky change, occasionally holding her breath as a shooting star zoomed across and out of the picture framed by her window. Occasionally, she'd wished upon a falling star—oh, nothing very important, usually fairly mundane. But last night, as she'd tried to calm the thoughts in her head, she'd found herself hoping there would be a falling star.

She'd actually wanted to make a wish, a highly impracticable wish… But there hadn't been a magic star…and now she was glad! Wasn't she?

She jumped out of bed, giving herself a little shake. She was being hopelessly romantic about Pierre and it had got to stop! She had to remain her own, independent, no-nonsense self. Anyway, Pierre was a once-bitten-twice-shy man so there was absolutely no point in getting soppy ideas.

She wedged herself in the shower and turned her face up to the warm cascade, screwing up her eyes and blotting out all unnecessary thoughts. She was looking forward to the day ahead, but she felt a certain amount of apprehension. Going out for dinner with Pierre, that was all very well—an extension of their early friendship—but working with him, that could be tricky.

For a start, their patient, Katie Smith. Pierre's *laissez-faire* attitude wasn't the one she would adopt if she were in charge of this case.

Pausing on the landing on her way downstairs, she decided to take a quick look at Katie. She tapped on the door and walked in. Pierre was leaning over the bed, one hand on Katie's forehead. He looked up, his eyes quizzical.

'Good morning. You're up early. I didn't expect to see you for hours yet.'

She approached the bed, noting that Mrs Smith wasn't in the room. She'd probably slipped out for some breakfast. 'I hate wasting the day. How's Katie? Did you detect any movement?'

He shook his head. 'I stayed a while with Mrs Smith last night to reassure her but—'

'You mean to assure her that she'd been mistaken, don't you?' Caroline blurted out before she could stop herself.

He drew in his breath. 'She was naturally disappointed that there was no recurrence of what she'd imagined—that's to say, what she'd thought had happened—so I stayed on to comfort her.'

Caroline took hold of the patient's wrist, feeling for the pulse which was one of the few indications that Katie was alive. She put her hand over the limp fingers, willing them to make some further sign of life. But there was absolutely no movement. She turned to look up at Pierre, blinking to remove the scratchy feeling in her eyes as she told herself this was a patient who was receiving all the treatment they could give and she herself must accept the inevitable. At the end of the day, as Pierre had told her, nature would take its course.

The last thing she should do was antagonise Pierre because…because he was her boss, and he was a very good friend, a very, very good friend who—

'Hey, don't look so sad!' He reached down and put the tip of his finger under her chin, tilting her face upwards towards him. 'You've been practising medicine long enough to cope with situations like this.'

She stood stock-still, her emotions quivering as she registered the touch of his finger on the sensitive skin of her face. Did he know how it was affecting her judgement? And, what was more to the point, did she herself understand what kind of transformation she was undergoing? It was something she didn't want to analyse, certainly not in a professional situation like this.

'Have you had breakfast?'

He'd removed his finger and she felt relieved to hear the mundane question.

'Not yet. Where…?'

'There's a small breakfast area we've created off the main reception. I think your grandmother used it as a sewing room.'

She smiled as her emotions calmed down. 'What a memory you have!'

He shrugged. 'I remember the ancient sewing machine. Your grandmother mended a seam in my old jeans one day. She'd noticed they were torn and suggested I bring them along. She lent me an old silk dressing-gown which had belonged to your grandfather, I believe, and I remember waiting in the kitchen, worried that you might come in from the garden and laugh at me.'

She laughed now, the amusing reminiscence helping to ease the tension. 'I don't remember that.'

'Why should you? Go and have some breakfast and afterwards I'll brief you about the work you'll be doing.'

She found coffee and croissants set out on a table in the

old sewing room. Jean Cadet was sitting by the window, spreading apricot jam on a piece of baguette. He stood up and moved over to the coffee-pot to pour out a cup for her.

She smiled as she accepted it and sat down next to him. 'Thanks.'

'I gather you used to live here. Must be very strange, returning as a doctor in a work situation.'

She broke off a piece of croissant. 'It is.' She popped the delicious morsel into her mouth, relishing the flavour and feeling as if she were home at last.

'Quite a challenge, I expect?'

'Not really,' she answered, unwilling to admit that, yes, she did have butterflies in her tummy about the work situation here. When she actually found out what was expected of her she was sure she'd feel easier.

'Have you met Monique?'

'You mean Pierre's ex-wife? Not yet.'

'Hah! That's a treat in store for you.'

She felt her spirits drooping. 'Why? What's she like?'

'She's absolutely— Well, talk of the devil!'

Caroline followed the line of Jean's gaze out through the window and automatically tensed as she saw the tall, slim, chic lady who was stretching her long legs from a white sports car, before pulling herself to her full height and hurrying across towards the main entrance.

Jean reached for the phone on the wall. 'Better warn Pierre that the enemy approaches!'

Now, that was more like it! This was how a divorced couple should behave. Caroline barely had time to wipe the croissant crumbs from her mouth with a blue cotton napkin before Monique was standing in the doorway, her mascara-outlined eyes swivelling around the room.

'Where's my husband?'

Caroline wanted to point out that Pierre was Monique's ex-husband but she remained quiet, pouring herself another cup of coffee. After all, they hadn't yet been formally introduced and for the moment she felt as if she were invisible. Maybe if she shrank a bit lower in the seat she would merge in with the decor.

Jean stood up slowly. 'Pierre will be here in a moment. Can I get you a coffee, Mme Chanel?'

Once again Caroline felt a pang of irritation that this woman should still be using her married name. Why hadn't she got married again or, at the very least, left her former husband to his own life?

'No, thank you. I have a busy schedule this morning.'

Probably at the beauty salon, Caroline thought, risking a glance at the immaculate make-up, the short, perfectly styled dark hair that snaked around Monique's ears and the couture suit clinging to razor-sharp hips.

'Let me introduce Dr Caroline Bennett,' Jean said evenly. 'Dr Bennett is going to—'

'Yes, yes, Pierre told me he was having to make a temporary replacement for Giselle. So inconsiderate of her to start a family so soon. I would have thought she'd have been more concerned with getting her career started. Can't think why Pierre appointed Giselle in the first place, considering she had a boyfriend and they were bound to get married and—'

'Good morning, Monique.'

Caroline was glad that Pierre's timely arrival had cut short Monique's diatribe. Another second of this odious woman's display of self-importance and she would have screamed!

'Good morning, darling.' Monique presented her faultless *maquillage* for Pierre's perfunctory brushing of the lips.

Caroline glanced at Jean, who raised his eyebrows in obvious agreement with her unspoken thoughts. Spare us the hypocritical endearments!

'If you'll excuse me, I've got work to do.' She wasn't sure where she was supposed to be working but anything was better than waiting around here in this disturbing scenario. She would make herself useful, go and see Katie or—

'No, don't go!' Pierre put a detaining hand on Caroline's arm. 'I'd like both of you to stay and hear what Monique has to say because it affects all of us here at the Clinique.' He turned to look at his ex-wife. 'You've come to discuss the financial situation, I take it?'

Monique frowned. 'Yes, but…' She glanced around at the captive audience. 'I was rather hoping we could go to your consulting room and—'

'Not a hope!' Pierre drew himself to his full height and treated his ex-wife to one of the icy stares he usually reserved for junior doctors who'd upset a patient. 'I'm in the middle of an important consultation with a patient so we'll have to have a brief discussion here. You went to see my accountant, as I suggested, I take it?'

'Yes, but he wasn't much help. I mean…'

Monique glanced at Jean. 'I think I will have that coffee after all, Jean.'

*'Bien sûr, madame!'*

The coffee was poured with a flourish and set in front of a now wilting Monique, whose initial bravado was evaporating by the minute. Caroline glanced around the small table where the four protagonists in this strange conference were sipping coffee and probably wishing they were elsewhere. Monique broke the awkward silence.

'Yes, I saw the accountant, Pierre. He was absolutely

no help at all. I told him I thought we should be making a profit by now and—'

'And I expect he reiterated what I'd told you—that this is not a profit-making establishment. We pay our own and our staff salaries, we take care of our patients and any surplus finance is ploughed back into the Clinique. You and I have the same salary, Monique, even though you are merely a sitting director, whereas I…'

Monique squirmed under Pierre's fierce gaze. 'Yes, yes, I understand all that but…' Again she glanced at Jean and Caroline who had both remained impassive throughout their boss's revelations. 'I really feel I would like a little more return for my capital investment in the château. If we were to increase the fees for our private patients—'

'Absolutely not!'

Even Caroline was frightened by Pierre's tone so what it was doing to Monique she could barely imagine. She watched the man she'd known as an amiable teenager turn into a tiger and she had to admit she rather liked him in this mood—especially when all the wrath was directed at his ex-wife!

'We've been through this time and time again, Monique! You know perfectly well that I have absolutely no interest in making money and—'

'Well, that's perfectly obvious!'

'Please, don't interrupt me!' he told his ex-wife, and her temporary bravado subsided. 'I became a doctor to care for the sick, not to make money. I opted to run my own establishment so that I would have more control in how I do this. When we first bought the château you agreed that—'

'OK, OK, I know I agreed to go along with your ideals, but that was when we were newly married and I wasn't thinking clearly.'

Caroline hated the sudden adoption of a coy, wheedling tone. She also didn't want to think about why Monique hadn't been thinking clearly when she and Pierre were first married. It wasn't pleasant to dwell on the fact that Pierre had brought his bride here to her château in the first flush of marriage.

'But now I have other obligations to fulfil. I've got my apartment in Paris and I've still got to finance my cottage in the village, for example, and…'

And your clothes and beauty requirements, Caroline thought bitchily, as her eyes strayed to the window. Suppressing a yawn, she detected that Jean was as incensed by this woman as she was.

A car came hurtling into the drive, gravel flying as the driver screeched to a halt. She tensed as she watched the car door open and an obviously distraught man lever himself out carefully, carrying a screaming child.

'Emergency!' Caroline said, relieved at the timely interruption but apprehensive of the difficult situation she envisaged when the small patient required their medical expertise. 'There's an injured child arriving and…'

There was no need to continue her explanation. Both Pierre and Jean were already going out through the door. Without a backward glance at Monique, Caroline joined them as they rushed towards the main entrance.

As the child was carried in through the wide open doors, Monique was disappearing towards her white sports car. She turned, briefly, to call out that she would phone later but no one acknowledged her remarks. All eyes were on the patient.

'Bring your little boy into my consulting room,' Pierre told the father in a kindly tone.

'I thought you told Monique you had an important patient in your consulting room,' Caroline said quietly.

Pierre glanced at her with a temporarily bemused glance. 'Tactics,' he muttered. 'Thanks for giving moral support.'

So that was why her presence had been required!

She turned away and looked up at the young father's distraught face. Got to give all her concentration to this potentially difficult case, putting aside all extraneous thoughts about Pierre and his obnoxious ex-wife, although she fleetingly reflected that she was glad Monique was obnoxious! The woman was decidedly attractive in a plastic sort of way, but her personality was such that Pierre couldn't possibly still have any feeling for her. Could he?

She found herself, briefly, wondering how on earth he could possibly have married her in the first place. Could it have been for her half-share of the money required for the château?

She put aside all extraneous thoughts as she prepared the examination couch in Pierre's consulting room. The little boy had stopped screaming and was staring up at her with terrified eyes. She judged him to be about two as she put out her hand towards him. He latched onto her fingers and begin to whimper.

She bent down towards him. 'What's your name?' she asked softly, as she began to unwrap the bloodstained bandage on his hand.

'Dominique,' the little boy told her as he loosened his hold on her hand so that she could get a grip on the bandage. 'My thumb's gone.'

# CHAPTER THREE

CAROLINE eased off the final section of the obviously home-made bandage. 'What happened?' she asked the trembling father, who looked as if he was about to faint as he looked again at the mangled thumb on his little boy's hand.

'Dominique was about to climb out of the car. He was in the back. He put his hand in the open door. His sister was climbing out of the front seat. She reached the pavement and slammed the door shut, without realising that Dominique's hand was there.'

Caroline swallowed hard to hold back her dismay at the mess which was the little boy's thumb. She could see the pulverised bone peeping through the skin and underlying tissue. Glancing across the examination couch at Pierre, she saw he was rubbing his chin, deep in thought. When he spoke, Dominique's father seemed to hang on every word, as if hoping for a miracle.

'I can operate immediately here, Monsieur…?'

'Monsieur Fleurie,' the father supplied quickly.

'…Or we can take Dominique to—'

*'Non, non, ici, immédiatement!'* M Fleurie pleaded anxiously. 'I've heard such good reports of this *clinique*. I prefer him to be treated here. Whatever the cost, I—'

Pierre put his hand out towards the father. 'The cost is immaterial. What is important is that we try to save Dominique's thumb. I will do my best but—'

'Oh, please, Doctor, don't amputate unless…' The young father glanced down at his little boy. Caroline was trying to keep him amused so that the discussion was going over his head.

'Dominique's sister plays the cello and his brother plays the piano,' M Fleurie continued quietly. 'His mother teaches piano at the Conservatoire de Musique in Boulogne. We have high hopes for Dominique. Already he can pick out tunes on the piano with his thumb…' The young father's voice trailed away.

Caroline had disentangled her fingers from the little boy's long enough to reach for a syringe loaded with a painkilling injection.

'What did you have for breakfast, Dominique?' she asked quietly as she injected his uninjured arm.

The little boy frowned as he tried to remember and it was his father who supplied the information which was required before an operation under general anaesthetic could be performed. Dominique had eaten very little about four hours ago so there wouldn't be a problem.

Caroline looked across the operating table at Pierre. His eyes above the green theatre mask had a worried expression.

'It's such tough luck that this should happen in a musical family,' he muttered half to himself as he surveyed the tiny unconscious patient. He glanced at Jean who, as a qualified anaesthetist, had given Dominique his general anaesthetic. Jean, carefully controlling the cylinders at the head of the operating table in the small theatre, looked tense.

'OK, let's see the extent of the damage, Caroline,' Pierre said in a noncommittal tone.

Carefully, Caroline peeled back the remaining skin to expose the underlying tissues and fragmented bone.

'The bone doesn't look too healthy,' Pierre said quietly,

making a gross understatement of the critical state of Dominique's thumb.

Caroline took a deep breath. 'No, but in a two-year-old child the bones are still soft. The healing process is easier than in an adult. If we were to immobilise the sections of bone and sew up the surrounding tissues and remaining skin we—'

'Now, why didn't I think of that, Professor?' Pierre said, the eyes above his mask showing his amusement at her presumption.

'Sorry, Pierre. You're in charge. I got carried away because I do so want this operation to succeed.'

'Pass me a sterile scalpel.' Pierre was deep in thought again as he leaned down close to the injured hand. 'As you suggested, Caroline, I'm going to sew up the tissues, after rearranging the bone splinters. Then I'll set the whole hand in plaster of Paris. We'll have to work on the thumb joint when the plaster comes off. As you say, the bones in a two-year-old are still soft so that's something to be thankful for.'

She held her breath. As Pierre began to work on the injury some of the tension in the room eased. Sewing up the skin at the end of his exploration and remedial work, Pierre asked Caroline to prepare the plaster of Paris.

She selected small bandages from the orthopaedic trolley, soaking them carefully in the required solution. After five minutes they were ready to be used on their tiny patient. She held the hand steady as Pierre fixed the plaster in position.

'I'll stay with Dominique until he comes round,' she said quietly.

'Shouldn't be long,' Jean said, making a final adjustment to one of the cylinders. 'He's had a very light anaesthetic because he's so young.'

Pierre was peeling off his mask. 'Give me a call when you've got him back in the children's section.'

As Jean had predicted, Dominique soon came round from the anaesthetic. Caroline held his uninjured hand as their resident porter wheeled him out of Theatre. Carefully, she placed him on one of the small beds in the children's section so that she could listen to his heart and lungs with her stethoscope.

Straightening up from her examination, she smiled down at Dominique. 'What a good boy you are. Would you like—?'

'I want my daddy!'

She smoothed back the damp, tousled blond curls from his forehead. 'Yes, of course you do. I'm going to call him right now. Would you like to press the buttons on the phone so that we can let him know where you are?'

She guided the tiny fingers of Dominique's good hand to select the digits. Reception came back almost immediately to say that they would send up Dr Chanel and M Fleurie.

'Daddy's coming now,' she told Dominique, settling herself on the chair at his bedside.

Glancing around, she saw that there were three other beds and two cots in the children's section. One baby was sleeping in its cot and the other was bawling its head off as a young nurse changed an abdominal dressing. The occupants of the beds were amusing themselves in the play area at the end of the room. From the happy noise that they were making, Caroline deduced that they were probably all convalescing.

She planned to have a thorough scrutiny of all their notes when she'd settled Dominique, who was now having problems adjusting to the fact that he couldn't put his favourite thumb in his mouth.

'Take it off!' he wailed as he rubbed the cold plaster against his mouth. 'I want to suck my thumb. Take it off!'

Pierre and M Fleurie arrived. Caroline was trying to explain to Dominique that the plaster was going to make his thumb better.

'Oh, dear,' M Fleurie said quietly. 'He's sucked that thumb since birth, I'm afraid. I know we should have weaned him off it but…' He reached for the good thumb and placed it against Dominique's mouth.

'No! My proper thumb, not that one!'

'He'll settle down soon, M Fleurie,' Pierre said in a kindly tone. 'I'll give him a mild sedative tonight so that—'

'Will he have to stay in?' Dominique's father wheeled round in surprise.

'It would be wiser.'

'He's never been away from home before.'

'We'll take good care of him,' Pierre said. 'And you can stay if you like. There's a bed in the next room that you can use.'

'I'll phone for my wife to come and then I'll go home to take care of the other children,' M Fleurie said.

Caroline felt relieved by this arrangement because Dominique's father looked all in. The shock had obviously taken its toll. She hoped the mother would be feeling stronger when she arrived. Meanwhile, she saw that Pierre was appointing one of the nurses to take special care of Dominique.

'Dominique's heart and lungs are functioning well,' she told Pierre as she walked with him down the corridor that led to the first landing. 'He's taken the anaesthetic in his stride. He's such a dear little boy. I do hope he's going to get the full use of his thumb back so that he can play the piano or the violin or—'

Pierre put his hand on her arm. 'Careful! You're becoming too involved. Nature will take its course with the healing of the bone and—'

'I wish you wouldn't keep using that phrase,' she said heatedly.

'Look at the facts!'

His hand tightened on her arm so that she had to stand still. 'We've done all we can to set the bone fragments in the right position, but it's dear old Mother Nature who will turn those fragments into viable bone—or not,' he added in a severe tone that gave Caroline the impression she was being ticked off by her headmaster. 'Agonising over it won't do anything to help the healing process,' he finished off, his eyes scrutinising her face as if checking her reaction to his words.

She leaned back against the window that gave light to the corridor as she faced Pierre.

'Tell me something,' she said in a carefully controlled tone which hid the confused emotions she was feeling. 'If you hadn't known me as a child, would you have spoken to me as you just did?'

Pierre raised one of his dark eyebrows as he looked down at her. He leaned forward and put one hand on the wall at the side of the window. She tensed, feeling that she was imprisoned in a small space which was totally enclosed by Pierre. It was not an unpleasant feeling—in fact, as she relaxed again she found the close proximity exciting in a deeply sensual way.

'What is more to the point,' he drawled, 'would you have spoken to me, your boss, in the way you did?'

In spite of herself she felt a slow smile spreading over her lips. Pierre could be infuriating but she found it impossible to be annoyed with him for long.

'Probably not,' she admitted in a resigned tone. 'Pierre…'

'Yes?'

She felt relieved that he'd raised himself to his full height again and was preparing to move off. It made it easier for her to try to think more clearly.

'It's an unusual situation we're in, isn't it? I'm going to find it difficult to adjust.'

'Me, too,' he said, his voice husky.

She looked up into the dark, expressive eyes, and felt as if a smouldering volcano were about to erupt deep down inside her.

'It's not easy for me either,' he said quietly.

'If I'd known you were in charge here I probably wouldn't have—'

'I'm glad you came.' He put a finger under her chin, tilting her face so that he could kiss the tip of her nose.

It was the lightest, shortest kiss in the most unromantic part of her anatomy but it sent shivers of excitement running down her spine. It must have affected Pierre, too, because he immediately became thoroughly professional.

'We'd better get a move on. I've got patients to see. You can sit in with me for the rest of the morning so that you get the hang of how we work our clinic consultations.'

At the end of the morning, Caroline felt she'd learned a great deal from Pierre. He'd explained that besides his private patients he had some patients who were funded by the state health system. Occasionally, he had to admit a patient, or send them to one of the appropriate hospitals. There were also visiting consultants on some days, who used the facility of their consulting rooms.

'We can have lunch here or take a few hours in the fresh air,' Pierre said in a casual voice. 'The clinic is usually quiet in the early afternoon and we're well staffed. I always insist we don't cut corners on the staffing situation, so what would you like to do? I feel I should take care of you for the first few days while you're settling in.'

She rearranged the pile of case notes she'd just organised. It was an occupation that meant she could keep her head down so he wouldn't see the annoying flush spreading over her cheeks.

'Oh, please, Pierre, I don't want any preferential treatment. I'm perfectly capable of—'

'I know, I know. And if you want to take your lunch-break on your own, that's fine by me. On the other hand, if you'd like to check out the bluebells at the top of the valley…'

'Oh, are the bluebells out?' Forgetting her resolve to stay professional, she was once again transported back to her childhood. 'I've always loved the spring here. In Hong Kong—' She broke off, embarrassed by her own childish enthusiasm. Pierre's face had an amused expression. Was he patronising her? She didn't care! It would be quicker to drive up to the top of the valley with Pierre than find her own way there. And he could be as patronising as he liked so long as she could gather some bluebells to set in a vase in her bedroom.

'Is this how you remember it?' Pierre was lying back amid the clusters of bluebells, with his back against the trunk of a broad chestnut tree.

'Yes, it hasn't changed at all!' Caroline said happily, as she knelt down to gather her bluebells. 'The trees seem smaller but that's because I'm bigger, I suppose.'

Pierre grinned. 'Not much bigger!'

She put the flowers down on the grass and aimed a mock

swipe at his head. 'As I told you before, diamonds come in little packages.'

He laughed. 'And poison comes in little bottles.'

'Why you…!'

This time he caught hold of her wrist as she aimed her blow at him, pulling her down beside him. 'Only joking! If you can stop picking flowers long enough we can have our lunch.'

He was pulling out packages from his rucksack and setting them out on a cotton tablecloth. 'I'll uncork the wine while you set some of this out. Mme Raymond has done us proud. I chose my cook very carefully when we first came to the château.'

'What was it like when you first moved into the château—with Monique?' she asked in a casual tone, as she unwrapped slices of ham.

Pierre pulled the cork out of the bottle and busied himself with searching for the glasses at the bottom of the rucksack. She could tell from the set stance of his shoulders that this was a question she shouldn't have asked.

'You mean, were we madly in love?'

'No, that wasn't what I meant. I was simply enquiring about the state of the château and how long it took you to get it to its present condition,' she improvised quickly. Was she so transparent, or was it that Pierre understood her too well?

Glancing at him now as he handed her a glass of red wine, she recognised the knowing expression on his face. She relaxed and allowed herself to smile.

'Well, were you—in love?' she said sheepishly.

'It was a long time ago. Does it matter?'

'No, of course not,' she said quickly. 'This ham looks delicious.' She passed the packet across to Pierre and he placed a slice on his disposable plate.

She took a sip of her wine and then another. Emboldened by the rush of false courage, she tried again.

'What I can't understand, after meeting Monique, is how you ever came to marry her. I mean, I wouldn't have thought she was your type.'

She heard his long-drawn out sigh and waited impatiently, hoping for some insight into the enigma of his unlikely marriage.

'What you see isn't what you always get,' he said slowly.

She picked up a prawn and began to peel it. 'That's a cryptic remark, if ever I heard one!' she said, trying to keep her tone light.

'I'm sure your grandmother and your mother would understand what I mean. I don't expect their husbands showed their true colours until it was too late.'

'Ah!' The light was dawning and with it a feeling of euphoria. There was absolutely no chance that Pierre would ever go back to his wife. She swallowed the prawn and rolled over onto her back, looking up at the curtain of leaves that shielded the sun.

'So why do you still have to make contact with Monique? I would have thought…'

He raised himself on his elbow so that he could look down on her. She noticed with alarm that his eyes were flashing fiercely.

'You always were an inquisitive child!'

'I'm not a child any more!' She tried to sit up but he put his hands on her arms.

'Surely it's obvious why I have to keep up a façade of friendliness with Monique. If she were to pull out her finances it would be disastrous.'

Caroline lay still while she digested this piece of information. 'You mean you absolutely couldn't manage? Couldn't you buy her out?'

'What with?'His voice spelt out the exasperation he felt at her futile questioning.

'I'm sorry. I hadn't thought the thing through.'

'Anyway, why the sudden interest in Monique? She's harmless enough if she's pampered and allowed all her creature comforts. So long as we don't antagonise her she'll continue to be a financial asset.'

'Has she got a job?'

'No,' he said with studied patience. 'Can we change the subject and—?'

'Just one last question,' she pleaded, and Pierre groaned. 'Where did she get her money from?'

Pierre gave a harsh laugh. 'Her first husband was very rich. When he died, he left everything to Monique in spite of the opposition of his grown-up children.'

He took away his hands from her arms and she sat up, trying out a conciliatory smile on him. 'Thank you for being so patient, Pierre. I do like to get to the bottom of things and—'

'You certainly do! Would you like another prawn before we pack up?'

He was already peeling it. 'Open wide!'

She laughed, almost choking on the prawn as he popped it in her mouth. It was one of the most sensual experiences she'd known. She swallowed and looked at the dark eyes so near to her face. His mouth was slightly parted. For some irrational reason, she hoped he would kiss her…

But he didn't. With what seemed to be a conscious effort he turned away and began packing up. 'Put the rubbish in this plastic bag.'

Talk about a let-down! She took a deep breath, before gathering the debris. Hadn't Pierre felt the frisson of sensual current that had been running between them just now? If he had he'd made it perfectly clear that he wasn't going to act on it.

Which was just as well, she thought as she stood up, brushing the crumbs from her skirt. Because she had no intention of allowing herself to get carried away on a cloud of passion with Pierre. Of all the people in the world, she wanted to keep her relationship with him platonic so that nothing would spoil their friendship—didn't she?

Back in the Clinique, after putting the bluebells in her room, she went straight to the children's section to check on Dominique. She found the little boy sitting up in his bed listening to his mother who was reading him a story. After checking that the plaster wasn't too tight on Dominique's arm, she reassured his mother, answering all her questions and explaining the treatment.

'You'll be able to take him home in a couple of days,' she told Mme Fleurie. 'We've inserted soluble stitches in the wound, but the plaster will have to stay on for about four weeks to ensure that the bone has knitted together again.'

'Will there be any lasting damage, Dr Bennett?' Mme Fleurie asked anxiously.

What a difficult question. Carefully Caroline explained that the injury had been a serious one. When the plaster came off, an X-ray would show how successful the treatment had been.

'I'm so hoping he'll follow in his brother's and sister's footsteps,' the anxious mother said. 'We have a cellist and a pianist so I was hoping Dominique would play the violin.'

Caroline swallowed hard. 'Well, we must never give up hope, Mme Fleurie. If everything goes well, there is no reason why Dominique shouldn't play the violin.'

'You really think so, Doctor?'

Caroline was suddenly aware of a towering presence beside her. As Pierre arrived at the bedside, his eyes told her he wasn't pleased with the way this consultation was going.

'But Dr Chanel will be able to be more precise,' she said quickly, passing on the responsibility.

The set line of his full mouth plainly said that he would discuss the situation with her later!

'We must be extremely cautious in our prognosis, Mme Fleurie,' he said in the deep, informative, professional tone he used for difficult situations. 'I won't be able to give you a correct clinical assessment until the plaster is removed. Meanwhile…'

He glanced at Caroline, and she was glad to see that his thunderous expression was somewhat modified. 'Meanwhile, we must hope for the best.'

'Thank you, Dr Chanel. You have all been so kind.' Mme Fleurie gave a faint smile. 'I have some teaching to do at the Conservatoire de Musique later this afternoon. Do you think you could keep a special eye on Dominique while I'm away? I'll hurry back as soon—'

'Dominique has his own special nurse to care for him,' Pierre said quickly. 'You don't have to worry about him at all. And Dr Bennett will be in this department all afternoon.'

'I thought it would be a good idea if you familiarised yourself with our young patients for a couple of hours,' Pierre said as they walked away to be out of earshot of Mme Fleurie. 'If we have an emergency then, of course, I'll page you but for the moment we're fairly quiet so…'

Caroline hated his smooth tone, the bland expression in his eyes. She may as well have been a young, unknown medical student for all the warmth he was giving out. What had happened to the effusive man who'd peeled a prawn and dropped it so sexily into her waiting mouth? They had to be professional on duty but was there any need to be quite so reserved with her?

'Pierre, I'm sorry if you didn't like the way I was handling the medical information I gave out to Mme Fleurie,' she said in a very subdued voice.

'Medical information!' he snarled. 'You were doing your optimistic best to eliminate any doubts about the outcome.'

Caroline glanced nervously across at Dominique's bedside where Mme Fleurie was closing up the story-book, preparing to leave.

'Well, I'm sorry if that's the way it came across,' she said quietly. 'I didn't think she would take me so literally. And I see nothing wrong in being optimistic.'

'That depends on the odds,' he said evenly. 'I'll see you later. You can page me if you have any queries about the children.'

For an instant she watched the tall figure striding away towards the door. Mme Fleurie was coming towards her, obviously completely unaware of the altercation which had occurred between the two doctors concerning her son.

'I've got to go now, Dr Bennett, but I'll be back this evening. I hope Dominique won't miss me too much.'

'Don't worry, Mme Fleurie.' There, she was doing it again! But she was only trying to keep this anxious mother's spirits up. She wouldn't be much good as a teacher today if she thought her child was bawling his head off. 'I'll go and read to Dominique for a few minutes so that we can get to know each other.'

Mme Fleurie put out her hand and touched Caroline's arm. 'You're very kind, Doctor.'

And very naïve at times, Caroline told herself as she

went over to Dominique's bedside. She couldn't help her innate optimism but she would have to be more professionally correct while she worked in Pierre's clinic.

There, she'd thought it! Pierre's clinic! That was the crux of the matter. She couldn't do as she liked here. This was no longer her home. It was a medical institution and she had to abide by the rules, defer to Pierre…

Well, she was only here for six months. She could surely cope with that for such a short time…it was a short time, wasn't it? It would soon pass. And then what? Go back to Hong Kong as if nothing had happened? Well, nothing had. Except she hadn't expected to have this awful turbulence of emotion coming out of the blue, just when she thought she'd got her life sorted out for good.

She reached down and smoothed back the tousled hair from Dominique's forehead. 'Would you like me to read you another story, Dominique?'

The little boy nodded and he grabbed the book his mother had left on the bedside table. 'Read the three bears again!'

She smiled as she opened up the French translation of the age-old story. Children the world over seemed to love it. Dominique's eyes were on her face, waiting for the story to begin. He pulled his plastered hand up to his mouth, intent on sucking his favourite thumb while he listened. Feeling the cold surface of the plaster, he frowned, then lay back resignedly against the pillows.

'''Once upon a time…''' began Caroline.

A few minutes later she became aware that Dominique's eyes were closing and then his breathing changed to the calm of sleep. Quietly, she closed the book and leaned over to examine his hand. Checking the end of the thumb that peeped out of the plaster, she reassured herself that the boy's circulation wasn't impeded.

She put the book down on the bedside table amidst the clutter of favourite toys, the bowl of fruit and the bottle of orange juice.

Helene, the nurse who was specialling Dominique, came across to take charge of him.

'Let me know when he wakes up, Nurse,' Caroline said, as she moved away to familiarise herself with the other patients.

The three children in the play area looked up apprehensively as she approached. 'We've had our afternoon rest,' one of them, a small, dark-haired girl said defensively.

'Yes, I'm not coming to put you back to bed. I just wanted to say hello.'

The little girl smiled. 'Hello, I'm Virginie. I've had my appendix out.'

The sister in charge of the children's ward had lifted a pile of case notes from her desk and was hurrying over.

'Dr Chanel said you would need these, Dr Bennett.'

'Thank you, Sister.'

She took the notes and put them down on a small table near the play area. She would make friends with the children before she studied their case histories. They were a happy little trio. The two boys, lively and full of energy, welcomed her help with the Lego house they were building, and the little girl, slightly inhibited by her sore tummy, remained close at Caroline's side, occasionally picking up one of the bricks and asking for it to be placed in a particular position.

When she finally got around to reading the notes, she was disturbed to find that Joseph, who was eight and very much the leader of the group, was suffering from leukaemia. He had been rushed in to the Clinique a couple of weeks ago for blood transfusions. He was now in a healthy state and would be going home soon. Caroline wondered how long it would be before he was rushed back in again. She made a mental note to ask Pierre if there was any possibility of a bone-marrow transplant.

Going on to the next file, she read that André, age seven, had been involved in a collision with a car. He'd fallen off his bike a couple of days ago and narrowly escaped being run over. Apart from concussion, he was uninjured. He was in the Clinique for observation and would stay there until the recurrent drowsiness subsided.

He didn't look very drowsy now as he fixed in place the last of the bricks onto his magnificent building!

'André, do you think you could break off for a few minutes so that I could see how you're getting on?'

'Sure.' André stood up and came over to Caroline. 'Are you going to start bashing my knee with that hammer thing?'

She smiled. 'I can see you're an old hand at medical examinations now.'

'I can't stop giggling when they tickle the bottom of my feet,' André said, as he climbed up on to his bed. 'Why do you do that, Dr Bennett?'

She leaned over the young boy, putting the light of her ophthalmoscope on. 'All the tests are to check that the messages from your brain are getting through. Now, do you think you could open your eyes wide? That's lovely.'

André was a patient child and extremely helpful. At the end of a few minutes she was able to reasssure him that he would be going home soon. As she said this she hoped fervently that she wasn't overstepping her authority! But all his reflexes seemed perfectly normal.

As she wrote down her findings on the notes she sensed that she was being watched. Looking up, she saw Pierre with Sister Janine. Ostensibly, he was discussing a patient, but his eyes had strayed towards her.

He smiled and she found herself relaxing as he came across the ward towards her.

'How are you getting on?'

'Fine! I haven't checked out the babies yet, but they're both asleep so—'

'Caroline, I'm sorry!'

He was speaking very quietly. She wasn't sure she'd heard him correctly.

'Could you repeat that?'

He gave her a boyish grin. 'Well, there's no need to make me grovel. I'm sorry.'

She smiled. 'That's what I thought you said but…' She paused, searching for the right words.

He put his head on one side as he looked down at her with a bemused expression. 'Did it seem so out of character for me to say I'm sorry?'

'No, no, of course not…well, perhaps a little. I mean, you can be a bit of a bully…even though you are the boss, of course, and—'

'Look, we can't talk here. Come down to my consulting room. We've got to get our working relationship sorted out.'

Caroline was aware that Sister Janine was giving them some very odd looks as she followed Pierre out of the children's ward, but she tried to keep her professional calm. Inside, the butterflies were flapping around. This could be make-or-break time; the start of an enjoyable six months—or the option to leave now.

'I don't want to lose you,' Pierre said, as soon as the door to his office had closed. 'You're a very dear friend and that's the trouble. It's always difficult to work with people you've known in a social situation. Especially if—'

'Especially if you've lorded it over them in a big-brother capacity,' she said quietly.

He put his hands on the side of her arms and looked down at her with a concerned expression.

'Did I do that? Did I lord it over you?'

Her eyes searched his face, touched by the complete lack of duplicity in his expression. 'I didn't mind then— I'd always wanted a big brother and you were fun to be with, but—'

'But now it's different,' he said huskily. 'I can't be your big brother any more because…'

He pulled her closer to him, so close that she could feel the beating of his heart through the thin cotton of his shirt. There was a faint aroma of an indefinably masculine scent, part body, part aftershave, but it played havoc with her senses.

'No, you can't be my big brother any more,' she agreed. The prospect should have made her sad, but instead she felt a sense of liberation. It was out in the open. The old relationship was over. They were ready to move on to…

Steady on, she told herself. Neither of them wanted to move on to the only other kind of relationship possible— did they? Pierre, as she kept reminding herself, had been well and truly bitten by his traumatic relationship with Monique and she herself had no wish to relinquish any of her independence, and yet…

His arms were tightening around her, making it impossible to think straight. She wanted to have a close friendship with Pierre but a no-strings-attached situation would be the only possibility. But what did he want?

Looking up at the tender expression in his eyes, she knew what he wanted at this very moment! But it was purely physical and surely he must recognise that, too. Her treacherous body was reacting to the feel of Pierre's muscular frame against hers. She ought to pull herself away from him but somehow…

When he bent his head and kissed her, she gave an audible gasp, which was immediately muffled by the touch of his lips. His kiss was casually light at first, but when it deepened and became more demanding she abandoned all attempts to analyse their relationship. The present was all that mattered. The wonderful sensual arousal that Pierre was provoking was impossible to resist. Her head told her to remain lucid but her heart was telling her to go along with the flow.

Suddenly, he raised his head and pulled himself away, his arms dropping to his sides.

'I shouldn't have done that.'

'I'm glad you did. It broke the ice.'

To her relief he laughed, a deep, good-natured sound that thrilled her almost as much as his caresses had done.

'I'm glad that's all it broke! I got carried away. I only brought you in here to apologise for being such a difficult person to work with. I'll try to respect you as a professional in future and not—'

'And not as a little sister.'

He moved closer again. 'I think we've broken that mould well and truly, don't you?'

'Absolutely!' It was off with the old and on with the new. But the new mould was going to be even harder than the old one to come to terms with. Still, it was going to be a fun experience!

# CHAPTER FOUR

IT WAS difficult to believe that a whole month had passed since Caroline had arrived at Clinique de la Tour. The bluebells at the bottom of the long garden had given way to roses and the heady perfume floating in through the open windows of the patients' rooms on the first floor was spoiling her concentration. It was the sort of midsummer day when she didn't feel at all like work.

She thanked her lucky stars that she'd chosen an interesting and absorbing career and that she wasn't confined to some awful desk job from nine to five. At least, being a doctor, it meant she didn't know what would happen each day. Some days she was rushed off her feet, and others were fairly quiet, like today. Nothing eventful was likely to happen this afternoon. There was a sleepy summer feeling both outdoors in the hot sun and inside in the air-conditioned cool.

How surprised her grandmother would be if she could come back and experience this feeling of enjoying a comfortable temperature all the year round! She thought back to the blazing log fire in the sitting room that meant you burned your skin directly in front of it and froze at the back. Central heating had been deemed to be a wicked and unnecessary waste of money. And in the summer the constant effort to keep the flies from the fields out of the château had meant that windows had often been closed, even in the height of summer, and it had been stifling indoors.

Glancing out through the window that looked over the

garden, she could see a couple of women patients sitting on garden chairs, deep in conversation. A nurse, in a thin white cotton summer uniform, had just given them some glasses of fruit juice and stayed to join in the animated discussion. Caroline wished she were out there, too. Working here in Katie's room, it could be so depressing. So much positive thinking was required not to come to the conclusion that this was a completely hopeless case.

She was glad she'd suggested that Katie's mother go out into the garden while she took these blood samples. The poor woman wasn't in the best of health after her weeks of sitting beside Katie, vainly hoping that there would be some reversion of the coma. She could see Mrs Smith now, at the bottom of the garden, walking by herself among the roses, occasionally stopping to examine one more closely, only the drooping shoulders indicating how depressed she was.

Caroline turned back and looked at the motionless figure in the bed. Katie must have been a pretty young woman. She checked herself quickly. It wasn't good to think of her patient in the past tense. Katie was still breathing, even though, after much heart-searching discussion, she'd been taken off the ventilator a couple of days previously. It was truly miraculous that she was still alive.

She crossed over to the bed and picked up the sterile syringe she'd prepared. The blood samples she was about to take would be used to test Katie's physical health. It was purely routine and she couldn't help thinking that at this late stage it was somewhat futile. All the neurological tests had pointed to the fact that there was no activity in the brain. And yet…

Looking down now at the peaceful expression on Katie's face, the long, dark hair endlessly combed and cared for by her mother, Caroline could imagine that her patient was simply taking a nap. She took hold of Katie's arm and turned it over, tapping on the forearm as she prepared a vein to receive the needle of her syringe.

She removed the required amount of blood and sealed it carefully away in a sterile container. Turning back to her patient, she started rolling the wide sleeve back to the wrist when suddenly she stopped and held her breath as she experienced a tremor of movement in the limp arm.

She sat down at the side of the bed and took hold of Katie's hand. 'Katie, can you hear me?'

There was no response. She'd imagined it. She felt positively foolish, getting excited about something that couldn't possibly have happened. How many times had Pierre told her that the neurological tests were conclusive? And yet…

She tried again. 'Katie, if you can hear me, squeeze my hand… Yes!'

This time she knew she hadn't imagined it! The faintest tremor of a movement came from the otherwise motionless fingers. She had to contact Pierre! Get him to see for himself what had just happened. Still holding onto Katie's hand, she picked up her mobile.

'I'd like you to come to Katie's room, Pierre,' she told him, as soon as he answered.

'Is it important, only I've—?'

'It's very important. Katie made a movement of her fingers. I—'

'Caroline, are you sure?' His voice was stern.

'Of course I'm sure,' she snapped back, annoyed that even now he didn't trust her medical judgement.

Over the past month their professional relationship had been strained at times but she'd hoped that things were improving. It hadn't been easy to work side by side, especially after the emotional reactions they'd provoked in each other during the first couple of days. Since that day when they'd picnicked in the bluebell woods and then, later, when Pierre had taken her in his arms and given her a most unprofessional kiss, they'd both made it quite clear that it wasn't going to happen again. And yet, underneath the professional exterior they were both striving for, she sensed the current of simmering emotions that occurred whenever they were together.

'OK, I'm on my way up.'

She breathed a sigh of relief as she turned back to her patient. 'Now, come on, Katie, don't let me down. I know you can hear me…at least I think you can. I'm sure I didn't imagine you squeezing my hand just now. Tell you what, try to open your eyes.'

She placed her fingers gently over Katie's eyelids. 'Katie, if you can hear me now, just open—'

Simultaneously with the door opening to allow Pierre to come in, Katie opened her eyes. Pale blue, bewildered eyes stared up at Caroline, unseeingly at first. Then, after a few seconds—in the time it had taken for Pierre to reach the bedside—Katie's eyes began to focus on her surroundings.

'Where…?'

The first, breathy, almost inaudible word that Katie had uttered since her accident seemed to hang in the air.

Caroline leaned forward so that she could hear every sound that Katie was making.

'Who…?'

Caroline could feel Pierre's hand on her shoulder, but she didn't look round. She could feel the hairs on the back of her neck prickling with the breathtaking excitement.

'Do you believe in miracles, Pierre?' she whispered.

'Oh, Caroline! There's always a medical explanation.' He removed his hand and leaned over their patient, whose eyes were now closed again.

'Katie, can you hear me?' he asked gently.

There was a flickering of the eyelashes but the eyes remained firmly closed.

He sat down on the edge of the bed. 'Can you squeeze my hand, Katie?'

Caroline saw the look of amazement on Pierre's face as he experienced a faint response.

He stood up, shaking his head. 'I can't believe it! So many medical experts have examined her and come to the same conclusion. It's nothing short of…'

He turned to look down at Caroline, who was holding tightly onto Katie's hand, positively willing her to come round again. She looked up at him and saw that his expression was distinctly wry as he searched for the right word.

'Miraculous?' she said, her happy smile counteracting the professional stance she was aiming for.

Pierre smiled back but refused to commit himself. 'I've read of rare cases like this where, against all the odds—' He broke off and raised his hands in the air in a gesture that indicated he was completely baffled. 'Now we need a concentrated treatment programme to speed up the recovery and—'

'Where…?'

Pierre broke off, his hand reaching forward to rest once more on Caroline's shoulder as they both waited for their patient to continue her barely audible question. Caroline heard the sound of the door opening behind her.

'It's lovely out there in the garden,' Mrs Smith said as she walked towards her daughter's bed. 'The roses at this time of year are— Katie!'

At the sound of her mother's voice, Katie had opened her eyes. 'Where am I?'

Sometimes, in later years, Caroline would recall the unbelievably joyous rapture that had swept over all of them, but at that moment she was too stunned to take it in. She knew she should stay calm, stay professional, but as she saw the tears rolling down Mrs Smith's face she had great difficulty in controlling her own tear ducts. Pierre, too, she noticed, brushed a hand over his eyes.

Mrs Smith had taken her daughter in her arms and was rocking her as if she were a child. One thing that worried Caroline was the fact that Katie was submitting to the embrace reluctantly. It was obvious that their patient had no recollection that this affectionate woman was her mother.

After a few minutes Pierre managed to persuade the delighted mother to relinquish her hold on her daughter so that he could test out Katie's neurological reactions. At the end of his examination he declared he was cautiously optimistic.

'Firstly, we'll have to build up Katie's strength. Let's try her with a few sips of water,' Pierre said. 'If she can swallow that we can proceed to semi solid, high-protein food. Then she'll need an intensive course of physiotherapy to restore her wasted muscles, and after I've contacted our neurological specialist we'll…'

Caroline could see that Pierre was thinking on his feet. He'd never experienced a case like this and he was plainly excited, even though he was trying to remain rational and professional. While Pierre had been outlining his plans for Katie, Caroline had contacted the nursing supervisor who sent up an experienced nurse to special their patient in her post-coma state.

Caroline picked up the feeding cup the nurse had brought with her. She half filled it with filtered water and, raising her patient's head, she put the spout of the cup to her dry lips.

'Drink this, Katie,' she said, trying to appear calm.

The dry lips latched onto the spout of the feeding cup and sucked in some of the water.

Caroline's eyes met Pierre's and she saw that he was smiling down at her. Maybe he didn't think it was a miracle, but she did!

'Dominique Fleurie has arrived to have his plaster off,' Caroline told Pierre, as she popped her head round his consulting-room door.

It was a couple of hours since Katie had come round from her coma. The whole clinique had been buzzing with the news. Patients and staff alike were in a state of excited shock but Pierre was doing his best to make it business as usual for the rest of the afternoon.

He was on the phone, but he cupped his hand over the receiver. 'Good! Take him into the treatment room and I'll join you there.'

As she closed the door she couldn't help overhearing Pierre say, 'Look, Monique, I've got to go now but...'

She tensed as she hurried away. Mercifully, she hadn't seen anything further of Pierre's ex-wife. That initial meeting had been more than enough for her. How on earth Pierre could bear to be in financial partnership with her Caroline didn't know! Still, if he needed her financial support... An exciting thought flitted through her mind. Supposing Monique did pull out. That would leave the field wide open for someone else to step into her shoes—financially. And that someone...

She put the tantalising idea from her mind as she walked across the reception area and smiled down at the little two-year-old.

'Lovely to see you again, Dominique. How are you?'

Trusting blue eyes stared up at her. 'Can I have my thumb back, Doctor?'

'Of course you can!' She glanced at Mme Fleurie, who was holding tightly to Dominique's good hand. At the back of her mind she knew she shouldn't be too optimistic about the outcome. There was a long way to go before they would know just how successful their treatment of the mangled thumb had been.

When Pierre joined her in the treatment room they settled their little patient on the couch. Mme Fleurie turned away as Pierre produced the rather alarming-looking sonic cutters.

'I think I'll sit over by the window,' she said in a faint voice.

'Why don't you take a stroll around the garden?' Caroline said gently. 'Dominique will be OK with us.'

Pierre flashed her a grateful smile. The last thing they wanted was a fainting mother when they were sawing through the plaster!

'I think I will, if Dominique doesn't mind…'

'Goodbye, Mummy!' the little boy said as he reached for Caroline's hand.

During the days he'd spent in the Clinique they had become good friends and Dominique had learned to trust her. When he'd cried on that first evening because he hadn't been able to suck his thumb, it had been Caroline who'd dried his tears and read him another story.

'OK, let's see what we can do,' Pierre said, as Caroline held Dominique's plastered hand firmly.

Carefully, he peeled off the fragments of plaster from the edges around the thumb and then, as gently as was possible with the cutters, he removed the whole plaster.

'There!' Pierre smiled down at Dominique. 'How does that feel?'

Tentatively, Dominique wiggled his whitish-pink, wrinkly-skinned thumb. 'It doesn't look like my thumb.'

'It's been all wrapped up for the past four weeks. It needs to get out in the fresh air,' Pierre told him solemnly, as he leaned over to inspect the scars formed by the sutures.

'Nice bit of stitching there, Doctor, if I may say so,' Caroline said.

Pierre glanced across at her and gave her a rather unnerving smile. She was doing her best not to become emotionally involved with this man but when he gave her that sort of look she felt positively weak at the knees.

'You may give me all the compliments you care to, Dr Bennett. A bit of approval never goes amiss, even in the medical profession—in fact, especially in the medical profession—between two colleagues.'

She swallowed hard. No need to go over the top, although she could see what he was getting at. Perhaps she'd overdone the professional attitude for the past four weeks. Maybe she should lighten up a bit—but if she did, where would that lead?

Remembering the emotions she'd experienced when Pierre had held her in his arms, she knew perfectly well where it would lead!

'See if you can bend your thumb, Dominique,' she said hastily, as she banished all the unprofessional thoughts. 'Very good! What do you think, Dr Chanel?'

'I think Dominique is a clever little boy. Now, I'm going to ask a nice lady to come and show you the exercises that will make your thumb really better. We'll ask Mummy to help you.'

When Mme Fleurie had been called back from the garden and the physiotherapist had finished her session with Dominique, Caroline went back to her consulting room. It was the smallest of the three that led off the old kitchen. She remembered when it had been the old television room, where she'd sprawled on the ancient, comfy sofa with the dodgy springs, cuddling one of the cats as she'd watched some all-intriguing children's programme. It had certainly been spruced up since the old days!

She'd agreed to vacate it for the use of visiting consultants but it was, nevertheless, the room she considered her own. It was a place where she could gather her thoughts and sort out her patients' case histories and treatment.

A computer dominated the main desk. She entered her reports on the patients she'd seen that day, before leaning back in the chair and switching off. Her eyes were drawn to the summer evening outside the window. She remembered she'd had no fresh air at all today. She stood up and stretched her arms above her head. A brisk walk up the fields was what she needed and then—

She recognised the light tapping on the door even before Pierre opened it.

'I came to see how you're getting on.'

He advanced somewhat warily into the room. Caroline could see that he wasn't sure if he was welcome or not.

'I was just planning to walk up the fields. It's such a lovely evening and—'

'Mind if I join you?'

'No, not at all.'

They were both being so painfully polite! She wondered how to break the ice. She gave him a tentative smile. He smiled back. Well, that was a start!

'Give me five minutes to change,' he said. 'Can't walk up the hill in this suit. It must still be hot out there.'

'I expect it is. I'll change into something cooler and meet you in the garden.'

She could see him sitting on one of the garden seats when she arrived back, after changing into a cotton skirt,

T-shirt and sandals. She thought how much younger, almost boyish, he looked in jeans and sweatshirt. A couple of patients strolling in the evening sun were mercifully leaving him in peace, probably realising that he was off duty for the day. He stood up as soon as he saw her approaching and came to meet her.

'Sorry I took so long. I couldn't decide—'

He grinned. 'Couldn't decide what to wear. Well, you made a good choice. You were worth waiting for.'

She could see he was in a good mood. Perhaps the temporary curtain was beginning to tear. Maybe he was feeling, like her, that a little rapprochement wouldn't do any harm. She fell into step beside him as they went out through the garden gate and across the path that led to the farm.

A huge, shaggy sheepdog rushed across the farmyard and barked madly. A man came out of the milking sheds, gave a friendly wave to Pierre and called loudly to his dog to stop the noise.

*'Tais-toi, Fanor! Veux-tu descend!'*

'I'm glad the farmer called off his dog,' Caroline said, as they began to climb the rugged track that led up the hillside. 'I expect it's a friendly creature when it gets to know you, but it's quite scary when it leaps up like that.'

'Only doing its job,' Pierre said. 'The highlight of its life is barking at strangers now there are no sheep to control. When my uncle owned the farm the dogs had work to do and usually dozed throughout the evening.'

'Who owns the farm now?'

'Monsieur Bouvier. His wife helps him with the milking and his three sons work in the fields. They're a nice family. Totally self-sufficient as far as labour is concerned, except for haymaking time.'

Caroline smiled. 'Ah, haymaking! I used to love helping your uncle.'

Pierre laughed. 'Helping, she calls it! The only person who was being helped was your grandmother. We got you out of her hair for a few hours.'

She paused on the upward track to catch her breath. All around her the calm of the summer evening seemed to have settled on the picturesque countryside. Only the birds were still calling to each other in the trackside trees, but the grassy fields lay still, not a breath of wind disturbing the tranquillity as far as the eye could see.

A rabbit, alarmed by their arrival, chased across a ploughed field and disappeared into the hedge.

'And I really thought my efforts with the drying grass were helping the haymaking team,' she said wryly.

'You were good entertainment value,' Pierre told her.

She looked up and decided she liked the expression in his eyes. She couldn't quite describe it as fond. It certainly wasn't admiration but it was something she couldn't quantify. But what mattered was that she enjoyed the warm glow it gave her.

Careful! she told herself. You're slipping towards that heady state you felt when he kissed you. If you stand here much longer he might try it again and you'd lap it up, wouldn't you?

She started off quickly up the track. Behind her the sun was casting long shadows over the hillside. If they stayed out long enough they could watch the sunset from the top of the hill. But she wasn't sure if Pierre had arranged for Jean to stay late at the Clinique. Her mind began to dwell on the patients again, even though she tried hard to immerse herself in the peaceful scene.

'That was a good job you did on Dominique's thumb,' she said, glancing sideways at Pierre.

He gave a self-deprecating shrug. 'As my father would say, most of the credit should go to Mother Nature. All I did was set the pieces of bone in a position where the healing process could begin. My father is an orthopaedic surgeon—he's retired now—and he always said that he was simply helping nature take its course.'

She smiled. 'Your favourite phrase again! Now I see where you get it from. But I didn't know your father was a surgeon.'

'My mother is a doctor as well. She's a paediatric consultant, in charge of the health of the children in several *arrondissements* in Paris. My parents have always been busy with their careers. That's why I was packed off to stay with my uncle, I expect.'

'Are you an only child, too?'

He nodded. 'We seem to have a lot in common.'

She liked the husky tenderness in his voice. It sent shivers down her spine. She couldn't help feeling like this when she was with him. Would it be so disastrous if they were to move their relationship on a stage further?

She turned to look at him and the heat rose to her cheeks. He was looking down at her with a distinctly probing expression. She felt utterly transparent, as if her wicked thoughts were written in bold letters just underneath her skin.

They had both stopped walking. He put his hands on her shoulders and drew her towards him with such tenderness that it took her breath away. She relaxed against his body, feeling the heat that seared through the thin cotton sweatshirt. Neither of them spoke. It was as if words would shatter the illusion that it was right for them to come together like this.

And then he bent his head and kissed her full on the mouth. Her lips parted in a rapturous reception. His tongue quivered next to hers. She could feel the strong vibrations of his muscular body as he held her close, his hands caressing the small of her back. And then, as if an unknown signal of agreement had been made, he pulled her down onto the soft grass beyond the verge of the track, cradling her head in his hands as he kissed her again, this time with infinitely more passion.

She pressed herself against his tantalising body, realising that he was aroused in a way that couldn't be satisfied except in the ultimate consummation. His hands were caressing her breasts; she could hear his excited breathing. They hadn't planned this; was she going to give in to the deliciously primeval urges?

As quickly as their passionate coupling had started Pierre pulled himself away, running a hand through his tousled hair as he leaned on one elbow and looked down at her with a wry expression in his sensitive hazel eyes.

'Caroline, what must you think of me? I didn't mean this to happen. I…'

She smoothed a hand over her crumpled skirt. 'You got carried away. We both did. I wasn't exactly fighting you off, was I? And I have to say…' She paused, shyly wondering how to phrase what she wanted to say to him. 'I have to say that I didn't want you to stop—but I'm glad you did.'

He sat up, tucking his shirt back in his jeans again. 'That's an ambiguous remark if ever I heard one! Would you care to explain?'

She smoothed back the stray hair that had fallen over her face. So much for the chic haircut! 'Oh, Pierre. You must have felt—sorry, unfortunate choice of words. Start again!'

He gave her a rakish grin as he sat up, bringing her back

against his chest, his arms supporting her like the arms of a chair. 'Go on, then. What am I supposed to have felt?'

She took a deep breath, trying to ignore the new tremors of excitement she felt. 'I think you must have realised I was reaching the point of no return and I was asking myself if I wanted to go all the way.'

'And what did you decide?' he asked softly, his mouth very close to her ear.

She turned round to face him. 'I hadn't come to a decision when you made the decision to stop. I didn't want our first time to be—' She broke off in embarrassment as he latched onto her words. She'd intimated that, at some unknown point in the future, they would carry on where they'd left off.

'I know what you're trying to say, that our first time should be in a special place—not out here in the fields where—'

'No, I wasn't saying that.' What was she saying? By using the phrase 'first time' she was practically committing herself to an affair with Pierre when that wasn't what she wanted…was it?

Looking up into his eyes now, her treacherous body was quivering with unconsummated passion. She knew that the surroundings made no difference to how she felt for this man. Against all her resolutions she was falling in love and this would spoil the delicate balance of their friendship. She wanted Pierre to remain her friend, not her lover. But from the way she'd behaved this evening she wasn't going the right way about it!

He hauled her to her feet, before standing back to brush the pieces of grass from his jeans. 'I would say you don't know what you want, Caroline. But I think I do.'

'I know I don't want anything to spoil our friendship,' she said quietly.

'Neither do I.' He dropped a kiss on the tip of her nose in that platonic way she'd relished until now.

For all her protestations she knew that their relationship had moved beyond the bounds of mere friendship. It was going to be difficult to handle the next delicate phase.

He held her hand loosely, almost companiably, as they walked back down the hill. Halfway down, he paused and pointed to the rosy glow of the sun disappearing behind the hill over the village. They watched in silence as the jagged, fiery tips sank lower in the sky until nothing remained but a pink and gold curtain that stretched over the top of the hills.

His fingers tightened on hers. It was a romantic moment which words would have spoilt, and they both seemed to realise this. She was glad they could share moments like this without analysing where their relationship was going.

Pierre released her hand as they walked in through the garden gate. The scent of the roses was everywhere. It had been an idyllic evening. She wished she could go on in this state of suspension, simply taking each day with Pierre at a time. Not looking too far forward, that was the answer. Enjoy the present.

'Are you hungry, Caroline?'

She smiled up at him, realising that, yes, she was ravenously hungry. 'I'd forgotten we haven't had supper.'

'I'll cook something.'

'Where?'

'In my own kitchen. Come on, let me show you!'

She followed him across to the old stable block. She'd been aware that he had some rooms here but she'd never dared venture this far without an invitation.

He stopped beside an ancient oak door.

'This was where all the cats had their kittens,' she said,

grinning as he flung open the door. 'Wow! What a transformation!'

'Does *mademoiselle* approve?'

'She certainly does.'

'And what would *mademoiselle* like for supper? The dish of the day is omelettes—or you could have omelettes.'

'The dish of the day, I think.'

'Have a look around while I phone across to Jean to see how he's coping.'

The rooms that Pierre had created were small but tastefully transformed. The building had always been referred to as the stables, by virtue of the fact that Grand-mère had kept a horse there in her younger days. But it had never been fully converted from the original old cottages. She was glad that Pierre had retained the original ancient fireplace in the first room which he obviously used as his living room.

Medical journals littered the coffee-table, the speakers from the CD player were cunningly hidden behind a large yucca plant and small landscape watercolour paintings had been slotted between the oak beams in the walls. Central to the room was the large, comfy-looking sofa set in front of the fireplace. The whole room gave off a cosy ambience.

Beyond the living room she found a small kitchen, which had been created by building a stone wall that remained uncovered by plaster or paper, thus lending an air of authenticity to the place. The bedroom would be upstairs but she didn't feel she should wander up there alone, even though it would probably be safer than asking Pierre to show her the way!

'I'm impressed by the high-tech pans on display, Pierre,' she said as he came into the kitchen, still clutching the mobile. 'How are things in the Clinique?'

'All quiet. Jean says he'll phone across if he needs either of us.'

'Ah, so he knows I'm here, too?'

He smiled. 'He asked where you were. Don't worry. He's very discreet.'

She bridled. 'There's nothing to be discreet about! We're having supper together, that's all.'

As soon as she'd said it she knew she'd set the parameters for the evening. Now she definitely wouldn't get to see the bedroom! Another time perhaps, another time when she'd sorted out her tangled feelings for this man who was stealing more little bits of her heart by the minute.

He was lifting down the omelette pan from its high shelf. 'Can you separate the whites from the yolks?'

She laughed. 'I'm a doctor, not a chef. That's cordon-bleu stuff, isn't it?' she asked jokinly.

'Not at all! Watch me. You crack the egg gently on the side of the bowl, conserve the yoke in the shell like this and allow the white to trickle down into the bowl. *Voila!*'

She perched on the edge of the rough old wooden table, dangling her swinging legs over the side as she watched him. 'Very impressive.' She ran her fingers over the ancient surface of the table. 'Where have I seen this table before?'

He was whisking the whites of the eggs with dedicated precision as if it were some kind of surgical procedure. 'I rescued the table from the garden. It's made of teak so it had survived and weathered the storms for many years out there, I believe. Pass me another bowl, please.'

Their hands touched as she gave him the bowl. She was trying so hard to remain platonic but it wasn't going to work. 'It's the table we had all our garden picnics on. It's quite high, isn't it? Let me find the cutlery and set it out.'

She placed her hands on the edge of the table, preparatory to jumping down, but he was too quick for her. His hands reached out for the sides of her waist, gripping her tightly as he lifted her down. They were dangerously close again, his lips hovering above her with tantalising expectancy.

The aroma of burning butter wafted over from the sizzling omelette pan on the wood-burning stove.

'Your pan, Pierre!'

Caroline didn't know whether she was relieved or frustrated by the timely interruption but later, as they relished the delicious omelettes together, she knew she would have to come to a decision one way or the other. She couldn't stand the emotional upheaval that was taking place in her well-ordered life. She'd planned a life of independence but all her resolutions were in danger of being broken.

Looking across the table at Pierre, his hair tousled, his face damp from leaning over the hot stove, his sensitive fingers pulling off another piece of baguette, she felt an almost irresistible urge to forget all her preconceived ideas about her future. But how would Pierre react if she told him how she felt? He, too, had very set ideas about where he was going in life and that didn't include committing himself to another person.

Maybe the answer was a light-hearted affair which didn't affect either of them emotionally? Who was she kidding? The depth of her feeling for Pierre was already more than she could handle.

'You're looking very serious, Caroline.'

'Am I? I—'

The phone rang. She relaxed as Pierre answered. 'I'll come over in a few minutes, Jean.'

'It's Mrs Smith,' he told Caroline. 'She'd like to see me about the fact that Katie still doesn't seem to remember her. I'd better go and reassure her. She's had a tough time during the last few weeks and I think she's almost shell-shocked by the reversal of the coma.'

Caroline nodded. 'Happy but bewildered, I expect. I'll come over with you—it's getting late. Do you want me to help you with Katie?'

He shook his head. 'No, the night staff are very capable. They know exactly how to make her comfortable for the night.'

They both stood. Caroline leaned across the table to gather up the plates but Pierre told her to leave the clearing-up.

'I'll do it when I get back. Go and have some sleep. It's been an eventful day.'

She swallowed hard. 'It's certainly been full of surprises. Katie coming out of her coma,' she added hurriedly. 'And—'

'And you and I walking up the hill together, getting to know each other rather more than either of us had planned, I suspect.'

The rakish grin on his face made him look madly boyish and desirable. If he took her in his arms now she would probably capitulate.

'Better go!' she said quickly, making for the door.

He arrived there before her, placing one hand at the side of the door so that he could look down at her. His expression was tender. She held her breath as their lips came together.

Was this the beginning of a wonderful, light-hearted romance or the shattering of a friendly relationship which could never be rekindled?

# CHAPTER FIVE

'KATIE has made a remarkable—dare I say miraculous—recovery!'

Dr Jacques Mellanger's words were like music to Caroline's ears. She glanced across Katie's bed at Pierre, wondering in a mischievous way if he'd taken exception to the word 'miraculous'. If he had, he was remaining quiet about it, deferring to the consultant neurologist's extensive knowledge and experience of coma patients.

Caroline ran her eyes across the chart she was holding. In the four weeks since Katie had come round from the coma she had certainly made lots of progress. All the tests were encouraging but there was a long way to go. She leaned down and smoothed away a strand of the long dark hair which had fallen over her patient's face. Katie gave her a wan smile and reached out with her thin arm to catch hold of Caroline's hand.

'Can I go in the garden, today, Caroline?'

Caroline gave her patient a sympathetic smile. Katie's voice still sounded somewhat ethereal, as if, having been snatched from the jaws of death she didn't really belong to this world yet.

'Dr Mellanger is the expert, Katie. Why don't you ask him?'

Katie's eyes widened with apprehension. Caroline knew Katie preferred to use her as a mediator. She was trying to make her patient a little more independent but perhaps she was expecting too much. It was still early days and she mustn't frighten the poor girl into going back into her shell.

Katie had no recollection of her former life and she had latched on to Caroline as her newest, most reliable and trusted friend. She'd even asked Caroline if they'd been friends before she'd had her accident.

Caroline looked up at the specialist neurologist. 'I think Katie would benefit from the fresh air and change of scenery, sir. Is there any reason why we shouldn't take her out in the garden in a wheelchair?'

The great man clasped his hands together and nodded benevolently. 'None whatsoever, Dr Bennett. So long as medical help is at hand in case of a relapse,' he added quietly.

Caroline felt a stab of concern. So far, Katie's progress had been excellent. She didn't want to do anything that would jeopardise this.

'Is a relapse a possibility?' she asked softly so that only the specialist heard.

He made a barely perceptible gesture towards their patient. 'Let's continue our discussion in your consulting room, Pierre.' He patted Katie's hand. 'Goodbye, my dear. Keep up the good work.'

Katie's eyes held a bewildered expression as she tried to detain Caroline once more with her thin hand. 'Are you going?'

'Yes, but Nurse Helene is here to look after you. I'll come back soon and take you into the garden.'

Looking back at the bed before she closed the door, she was rewarded by the sight of Katie's happy face.

Down in Pierre's consulting room the three of them settled themselves to pore over Katie's case notes and the results of her extensive neurological tests.

Dr Mellanger pushed his longish grey hair back behind

his rather large ears, balanced his half-specs on the end of his aquiline nose and cleared his throat, as if he were preparing to give a lecture.

'As I said before, a remarkable case. I'm deeply indebted to you, Pierre, for calling me in on this one. As you know, I'm writing a paper on coma patients who've recovered against all the odds for the autumn conference of neurologists in Paris and Katie will feature in it—with your permission, that is.'

Pierre leaned across his desk and nodded. 'Of course.'

Caroline shifted in her chair at the other side of the desk. 'What I can't understand is how Katie could have appeared to be brain dead for...' she glanced down at the notes '...approximately ten weeks, and recover the majority of her faculties. To me, it seems nothing short of a miracle.'

She allowed her eyes to meet Pierre's across the desk. A glimmer of a smile lit up his face. They'd agreed to differ on this one but his sense of humour was still intact.

In fact, it was a sense of humour and general *joie de vivre* that was the basis of their relationship at the moment. It was as if both of them were treading on eggshells, maintaining a fragile attempt to keep up a pretence that a platonic relationship was what they wanted. Neither of them seemed ready to make a further commitment but Caroline recognised that behind their light-hearted banter they were hiding their real feelings for each other. At least she was— she would have loved to know exactly how Pierre felt about her.

Dr Mellanger cleared his throat and Caroline focused all her attention on the expert once more.

'A miracle is certainly how it would seem. The fact of the matter is, in spite of extensive research, we're all still searching for conclusive answers. The most rational explanation that I can come up with is that the brain simply shuts down after a traumatic accident. When tests are performed, no visible sign of activity is recorded. If the coma continues for a number of years then the deterioration of the brain and body cannot be reversed. But occasionally, after a matter of weeks—usually in a young, previously healthy person—the brain, after its recuperative sleep, starts to function again.'

Pierre stood up and walked over to the window, leaning his back against the warm sill as he swung round to question Dr Mellanger. 'What is the possibility of Katie recovering her long-term memory?'

The consultant frowned. 'I wish I could answer that one but all the cases I've studied have varied. Sometimes there is a sudden flash of memory of previous experiences. In many cases the long-term memory doesn't return and the patient has to start life afresh as if they were a child, learning all the skills they once knew.'

'Katie becomes so frustrated by little things, like doing up the buttons on her nightdress,' Caroline said.

'Quite so. This is where we have to rely on great patience from all the medical staff.' Dr Mellanger glanced at his watch. 'Unless you have any more questions, I must be getting back to Paris.'

Caroline stood at the main entrance with Pierre, watching until Dr Mellanger had safely negotiated the other cars parked out front and had set off down the drive.

'Most enlightening,' she said, as she turned away to go inside. 'I'll take Katie into the garden. If she settles OK, I could get Helene to sit with her, otherwise—'

Pierre put his hand on her arm. 'It's better if you stay with her, Caroline. We can't take any chances. And you're the one she trusts the most. Even her mother has stopped visiting so much now that she can see Katie is getting full, round-the-clock attention.'

'I really wanted to work in the children's ward this morning. Joseph's new medication needs sorting out. Since he got back here from hospital after his bone-marrow transplant, I've been trying to spend time with him each day to observe how the treatment is having an effect on him. I'm not altogether convinced that the new medication is working as effectively as it should.'

'I'll go up and make some observations myself and we'll compare notes later,' Pierre said. 'But your main priority at the moment is Katie.'

'So it would seem.' She didn't begrudge the time she spent with Katie but she felt that her patience was often stretched to the limit.

'How about lunch? What had you planned today?'

She felt a frisson of excitement. They hadn't had a lunch date since that day in the bluebell woods. Was he planning something special or was it simply joining the rest of the staff in the dining room?

'Hadn't given it a thought. If Katie starts to throw a wobbly…'

'Get her back to bed before lunchtime. She'll be tired by then. Jean can hold the fort and we'll go off to Le Touquet for a few hours. This weather is too good to waste. Bring a swimsuit and a towel. We'll have a swim before lunch.'

She laughed. 'Any more instructions, sir?'

He touched her under the chin, lifting her face towards his. 'No, that will be all for the moment, Dr Bennett.'

She was desperately aware of the startled glance that the nurse at Reception was directing towards them. Abruptly she turned away, fighting to control the pink flush that she could feel spreading over her cheeks.

As she walked up the stairs to the first landing, she reflected that Pierre was hopeless at hiding the fact that there was something going on between them. Was he testing out how things would be if they really did start having an affair? Was this occasional public show of closeness a ploy to see how she would react?

She put the complicated thoughts from her mind as she opened Katie's door. The big smile on her patient's face was reward indeed. She felt humbled and honoured that she could devote some time to this worthwhile and remarkable case. The experience she gained from working with Katie would be something she never forgot in her future medical career.

Returning Katie to her room at the end of the morning, she didn't feel quite so enthusiastic. Katie had been querulous and exacting in the garden, demanding to be wheeled around for most of the time and refusing to wear her sunhat. She was just like a child but with an adult's body and self-will.

For the final half-hour, Caroline had parked the wheelchair under a large tree and had spent the rest of the time teaching Katie to read. She was learning more quickly than a child but not quick enough for her own satisfaction. Time and again as she stumbled over a word that Caroline had taught her the previous day she gave a howl of frustration, finally closing the book over Caroline's fingers and starting to cry.

Caroline had comforted her, knowing that her patient was tired and would sleep when she'd had her lunch.

Helene helped her to put Katie back into bed. Mme Raymond, the Clinique cook, a large, capable woman with plump arms, arrived with a tray and set it down on Katie's table. The *chef de cuisine* didn't usually deliver meals in person but when it was a star patient like Katie she was curious to know how she was getting on.

'What did the specialist have to say about Katie?' Mme Raymond asked, with all the authority of a specialist herself.

Caroline spent the next few minutes giving a report while Helene got on with helping Katie to eat her lunch. She knew that the kind-hearted cook was very concerned with Katie's progress. As soon as was decently possible, without appearing rude, she glanced down at her watch and admitted that she would have to leave.

Mme Raymond clasped her hands across her ample bosom. 'Sorry, dear, I'd forgotten you were going out for lunch.'

Caroline's eyes widened. 'Yes, well…'

'Dr Chanel gave me all the instructions. You won't go hungry this lunchtime, I can tell you. Where is he planning to take you? I presume it's you who's going because he did say a picnic for two so—'

'I really couldn't say, *madame*. Wherever it is, I'd better be off! Goodbye, Katie. Have a sleep and I'll see you later.'

It was a conspiracy! Pierre was forcing her hand. He wanted to know how she felt about him.

As she climbed into the passenger side of his car, she asked herself exactly how she did feel about him—apart from confused, that was! Why couldn't she accept that she was falling in love and go along with the delicious feeling that kept stealing over her? Was it that she still resented the fact that Pierre had stolen her château from her? Did she still bear him a grudge? Or was it that she didn't want to risk a casual affair that might mean too much to her? Would it be heartbreak time when she had to leave Pierre and the château behind and go back to Hong Kong?

She glanced sideways at Pierre's strong profile, his hands holding the steering-wheel, his mouth set in a firm line above the determined jaw. He seemed to be in a world of his own at the moment, not speaking or communicating with her at all. She would love to see inside his head and find out what he thought about her!

She settled back in her seat and closed her eyes. A few moments of sheer relaxation would be most welcome after her long morning.

The beach at Le Touquet was fairly quiet. It was still only July and the August rush to the coast hadn't yet started. A sprinkling of people walked by the water's edge. The tide appeared to be coming in.

She'd put on her bathing suit before leaving the Clinique, so all she would have to do would be to drop her sweater and jeans in a heap. She was carrying spare panties and a towel in her large holdall. Pierre had a huge picnic basket, the sort she'd once taken to her grandmother at Christmas full of goodies from Fortnum and Mason in London. It looked very heavy, or perhaps Pierre's exaggerated movements were meant to draw an expression of sympathy from her.

'You won't be able to stagger·very far with that basket,' she said wryly, as he locked up the car.

'Nonsense! We'll go along the top of the beach and find a sheltered spot among the sand dunes.'

'Why didn't you bring the rucksack, like you did last time we had a picnic?'

He grinned. 'Because this is a special picnic, not simply a few bits of baguette thrown together with ham and to-matoes. I gave Mme Raymond instructions about what the picnic hamper should contain.'

'I know, she told me.'

'Ah!' He gave her a searching look. 'Do you mind?'

She adopted a totally innocent expression as if the thought had never crossed her mind. 'Why should I mind?'

He was several feet in front of her already, carrying the heavy basket in front of him. 'Mme Raymond does tend to jump to conclusions.'

She caught up with him. 'Such as?'

He laughed. 'Stop winding me up, Caroline! You know perfectly well that she'll talk and the grapevine will be of the opinion that there's no smoke without fire.'

She took a deep breath. 'So when does the fire start?'

Had she really said that? It was almost as if her sub-conscious had taken control and banished all her inhibitions. She held her breath as she waited for his reaction.

He stopped in mid-stride, dumping the heavy picnic basket down on the side of a dune. 'Whenever we light the match,' he said huskily.

Leaning forward, he took hold of her by the waist and brought her against his chest, his arms cradling her back. She looked up at him and relished the tenderness in his eyes.

'Pierre, I'm so afraid that if we light the fire it will get out of control and neither of us wants to have a huge furnace on our hands.'

He gave her a rakish grin, his expressive eyes studying her face.

'It's easier to talk in metaphors than be direct with each other, isn't it? But, seriously, Caroline. I've given our relationship a lot of thought and I don't see why we can't accept that we're both attracted to each other in more than a just good-friends way. I'd love to forget all about the fact that we knew each other years ago in a completely different life. If I'd only just met you for the first time, I'd be making plans to seduce you as soon as I felt the faintest frisson of a response from you.'

She swallowed hard as conflicting emotions churned through her. 'And after the seduction, what then? You wouldn't expect me to capitulate all my independence and—'

'Good heavens, no. I understand you completely. A little light-hearted affair would ease the tension between us, don't you think?'

She gave him a long, slow smile. 'I'm trying not to think, to be honest. Come on, let's keep walking.'

Walking beside him through the dunes, she felt a light-hearted sense of happiness stealing over her. Pierre was right. They had to forget that former life they'd spent together; view each other as new people and have a no-strings, fun affair, where nobody got hurt when it was over because it was what they'd both agreed on.

Pierre dumped the basket down in a hollow created by a circular sand dune. 'Phew! I need a swim to cool off.'

He was already stripping off to reveal black swim trunks under his jeans. She peeled off her clothes, dropping them in a pile on the sand. He was waiting for her to finish, his hand held out towards her. She took hold of it and together they sprinted down the sand. The feel of his fingers clasping hers added to the light-hearted, happy feeling that was enveloping her.

The water felt cold as they ran into the rippling waves. Pierre immersed himself immediately and, as Caroline held back, he splashed water on her. Screaming at the cold shock, she chased after him. For a few seconds he swam away from her and she knew she hadn't a hope of catching up with him. Turning over onto her back, she looked up at the wide stretch of blue sky and the fluffy clouds, scurrying round the sun like cotton-wool balls.

Mmm! This was the life! She could take more of this.

She froze as something brushed against her thigh. 'Pierre! I thought you were a shark!'

'No sharks around here! I'm very friendly,' he said, as he surfaced from the depths right next to her.

'Over-friendly, I would say.' She laughed as she trod water, trying to cope with his arms around her shoulders drawing her towards him.

His kiss was light, but exciting enough to take her breath away. 'Pierre, I'm not such a brilliant swimmer that I can handle this situation in deep water.'

'Don't worry. I'm trained in life-saving and the tide's actually sweeping us in towards the shore. We can catch the next wave, like this…!'

Still holding her hand, he pulled her with him as he dived into a wave which carried them along and flung them into the shallows. Caroline staggered to her feet, laughing with exhilaration. He caught her in his arms and smoothed the hair out of her eyes.

'We should relax like this more often,' he said, grinning.

'Relax, he calls it! I feel like a beached whale.'

'Quite a good description, if I may say so.'

'Why, you…!'

She chased after his athletic form but it was impossible to catch up with him until she reached the sandy hollow where they were to have their picnic. He tossed her a towel.

'Better do something with the seaweed on top of your head!'

He was grinning and she knew he was trying to lighten the emotional tension by making fun of her. As she rubbed her hair vigorously she was trying to calm down, to tell herself not to go overboard emotionally. Take one step at a time and—

'Here, let me do that for you.' He reached forward and

took the towel from her hands, smoothing it slowly over her wet hair. Then, dropping the towel round her shoulders, he ran his fingers through the tangled knots, gently teasing them out before beginning a slow massage of her scalp.

'Lean back against me,' he said quietly. 'This will relax you after all that exertion.'

Her knees felt as if they would buckle under her as she leaned back against his bare chest. His fingers were pressing soothingly against her head, moving in a slow, rhythmic motion that was beginning to drive her wild with mounting excitement. It was one of the most erotic movements she'd ever experienced! Standing there among the sand dunes, just by the movement of his fingers Pierre had created the background for an impossibly sensual encounter.

Impossible because, glancing round at the strolling holidaymakers and family groups, she knew there was no way Pierre could satisfy the deep desires welling up inside her. She would have to contain herself for another time, another place.

She swung round to face him. 'Thanks, Pierre. I think my hair—'

His kiss silenced her. As his lips claimed hers she gave a sigh of compliance. This was what she had hoped for. But even as his kiss deepened she knew that she mustn't go along with the tidal wave of her emotions. Pierre, too, seemed to realise that they had to remain sane and not get carried away.

His eyes were darkly expressive as he pulled away. She looked up at him, her lips tingling with the salt taste of him and her body throbbing with desire.

'I think we'd better come down from the clouds and have that picnic,' he said huskily. 'Unless you'd like to pack up and we could register in a hotel for a couple of hours?'

'No!' Her response was swift and automatic. A couple of hours in a hotel was not what she wanted for the love that was welling up inside her.

'I'm sorry, I didn't mean to compromise you.' He put his hands under her chin, cupping her face so that she had to meet his agonised gaze. 'I would never do anything that we didn't both want. I won't ever suggest—'

'Please, Pierre!' Panic was setting in. She didn't want to lose the ground she'd gained by appearing totally unwilling. 'That wasn't what I meant. I'd just prefer that the first time we…'

He brushed his lips across her cheek. 'So should I. I know what you're trying to say and I agree entirely. A romantic weekend for two, somewhere away from familiar surroundings, away from wagging tongues and—'

'Well, I hadn't thought that far but—'

'I know the perfect place. My favourite hotel in Normandy. How about next weekend?'

Events were moving too quickly for her! The whole idea was simply blissful but the implications were too serious to consider as she stood next to him, her skin still damp from the sea, her head tingling with the memory of that erotic massage.

'I know, you need time to think about it. I won't rush you. Let's have lunch.'

His voice was brisk, almost professional as he turned away and began to unpack the contents of the basket.

She spread a towel on the ground, curling her sandy feet under her as she watched Pierre uncorking a bottle of chilled white wine.

'It's still cold,' he said, as he adjusted the chilling plastic wrap-around case that surrounded it.

He was smiling again as he handed her a wineglass.

'Delicious! Most refreshing,' she told him as she took her first sip. 'I'd like to propose a toast.'

As she held her glass towards him she could feel her fingers trembling. It was now or never. She couldn't keep shelving the issue. 'To a romantic weekend away from it all!'

His smile broadened as he clinked his glass with hers. 'I'll drink to that.' His eyes were tenderly expressive. 'Let's unwrap some of these packets and see what's for lunch.'

'Mme Raymond has really done us proud!' Caroline said as she munched her way through a piece of asparagus quiche.

'Try the smoked salmon. It's very good.' He held out the plate towards her.

Their fingers touched as she selected a small section and she felt a thrill of excitement. The thought of a whole weekend with Pierre was almost too much to contemplate. A tiny, niggling doubt was trying to spoil her delicious anticipation. Didn't it all seem too blissful? What about when she had to leave all this behind?

'You're looking all serious and worried again.' His deep, gravelly voice interrupted her thoughts. 'What's the matter? Having second thoughts?'

She smiled. 'Certainly not. I shall enjoy a weekend away from the Clinique. But how will we manage, staffwise I mean?'

'Leave the planning to me, Caroline. I'll sort out the staffing situation. All you have to do is pack a small week-end bag and be your own delightful, charming, irrepressible, sometimes infuriating—'

'You really know how to get round a girl, don't you?'

He laughed. 'Not any girl. But I think I understand you more than most. I've known you long enough.'

She had another sudden stab of doubt. 'Yes, but I've changed a lot during the time we were apart.'

He gave her a rakish grin. 'Thank goodness! I certainly wouldn't want to spend a weekend with a difficult, obstinate, willful—'

'Hey, come on! I wasn't that bad, was I?'

'You were a bit of a handful at times. I sometimes felt relieved when it was time for you to go back to the château.'

She lay back against the sandy bank and closed her eyes. 'The château,' she murmured. 'Sometimes I dream it's still the way it used to be. How I loved it as a child—still do, but it's not the same.'

His arm came stealing around her shoulders and he drew her against him. 'Have I spoiled your dream for you?' he asked gently.

She sighed. 'I have to admit, I'd always imagined I would live in the château—as it was in Grand-mère's time. But it was only a dream. Life has moved on and—'

'I asked if you resent the fact that I bought the château when you wanted it?'

His voice was steely calm and she could feel the rigidity of his arm as it touched her shoulders. She didn't want to spoil their deepening relationship but, then again, she couldn't go on hiding this important fact from him.

'I've tried not to worry about it,' she said quietly. 'When I first arrived and found out who'd pipped me at the post I must admit I did resent it. But I could never hold a grudge against you, Pierre.'

She turned her head and looked up into his eyes. He lowered his head and kissed her cheek. 'I'm glad you're being honest about it. It's worried me ever since you told me you'd wanted to buy the château.'

'The only thing that worries me about the situation now is the fact that your ex-wife owns half of it.' She spoke quickly, before she had time to keep her opinion to herself.

He pulled his arm away and sat bolt upright. 'Caroline, I've told you that without Monique's investment I couldn't have afforded to buy the château. She may be a pain but at least she's financially solvent so…'

Was this the moment to put forward the mad scheme which had been formulating inside her head? Supposing she were to offer to buy Monique out? She glanced sideways at Pierre but his enigmatic eyes didn't encourage her to voice her idea. It was too big a project and she had to think it through.

Firstly, Monique might not want to be bought out; secondly, a financial alliance with Pierre might be the kiss of death to their relationship; thirdly…

'You've gone all quiet again. You're miles away from me.'

She took a deep breath. It was now or never. She couldn't keep quiet about something so close to her heart. She'd share her mad idea and think about the logistics of the situation when she'd heard Pierre's opinion.

'I was wondering if it would ever be possible for you to take on another financial partner,' she began tentatively, trying desperately to keep her voice steady. 'I mean, from what I've seen of Monique, she doesn't seem too happy with her investment. And I would have thought you'd be glad to get rid of a financial alliance with your ex-wife. So, would you consider…?'

'No! Don't even think about it, Caroline!'

She stiffened as she heard his sternly negative reaction, pulling herself away so that she could remain calm.

'Why?' she heard herself say in a voice that was little more than a whisper.

'Because…because…' He held both hands up towards the sky as if it was the most hare-brained scheme he'd ever heard. 'Don't think I'm not grateful that you would consider making an investment in the Clinique, but it just wouldn't work—for a number of reasons.'

'Which are?' She was getting bolder by the minute! Having gone this far, she wasn't going to be fobbed off.

'Because you'll be going back to Hong Kong and, anyway, I'd never consider putting myself in the same position as I did with Monique. Never mix business with pleasure.' His eyes held a veiled, enigmatic expression as he turned towards her. 'Let's leave things as they are, Caroline.'

She noticed that his voice was gentle again. Reluctantly, she moved towards him.

He pulled her against him and she tried to relax. A cloud passed across the sun and she could feel the delicious feeling of rapport evaporating. She had to live in the real world again, not the make-believe fantasy she'd been creating. Reaching for her towel, she pulled herself away from his arm and stood up.

'I'm beginning to think about work again,' she said, brushing the sand from her feet as she slotted her toes into her sandals.

'Best to keep your feet on the ground,' he said quietly, as he began assembling the picnic debris.

She thought back over their discussion. Pierre had known what she was going to say even before she'd plucked up courage to air her views. Had he been reading her mind for some time now, expecting her to voice her scheme? No, that was impossible. But he certainly did seem to have second sight where she was concerned.

'Here, let me help you, Pierre.'

'That's OK. You get dressed and then we'd better set off back.'

As she pulled a T-shirt on over her bikini top she was hoping that she hadn't put Pierre off the idea of their weekend in Normandy.

# CHAPTER SIX

A COUPLE of weeks after their picnic in the sandhills of Le Touquet, Caroline was beginning to think she'd imagined the tender, sensual emotions they'd shared on that day. Pierre was continuing to treat her as a valued colleague and friend but she felt no nearer to understanding his feelings for her than she had during the first weeks of her time at the Clinique.

Hurrying down the stairs from her top-floor room, she paused to look out of the window. Pierre was running down the path from the fields, his hair tousled around his face, his arms moving in a strong rhythm with his muscular legs. Even from this distance, she could see the sweat gleaming on his suntanned body. He looked good in running kit, black shorts and white cotton top. She'd seen him looking like this on numerous mornings, pursuing his fitness regime, and it always turned her on!

She turned away. Better get on with some work! She liked to see a few patients before breakfast and check that things were running smoothly after being off duty all night. The three resident doctors, Pierre, Jean and herself, shared the night calls. The night nursing staff were pretty efficient and it was rare to be called from her bed, but she always had a better night's sleep when she knew there was no chance that the telephone would ring.

Katie was always her first priority in the mornings. She found her patient sitting by the window, enjoying a croissant liberally spread with apricot jam.

'Hello, Katie. How's life treating you today?'

'Caroline!' Katie put down the croissant, licked her fingers and held out her hand. 'Come over here. Come and see Dr Pierre running down the garden.'

Caroline took her time as she crossed the room.

'Oh, you've missed him. He's gone inside. He looked so handsome!'

'Did he?' Caroline said in an innocent voice, deliberately standing with her back to the window.

'Oh, you know he did! You must have noticed.'

'I suppose he is. Now, if you're feeling OK and there's nothing worrying you I'll—'

'Oh, but there is something worrying me,' Katie said quickly.

Caroline waited for Katie to dream something up so that she would have to stay longer. It happened all the time now, but she was relieved that her patient was well on the way to recovery.

'It's the *son et lumière* show in the grounds of Montreuil castle tonight and I'd love to go and see it. Mum says I went last year but, of course, I don't remember and I've heard it's so beautiful. Will you take me, Caroline?'

Caroline hesitated. 'It's a late start, Katie. Ten o'clock, I believe, so we wouldn't be back until after midnight and—'

'You sound just like my mother! She said I had to ask if you would take me but she didn't hold out much hope.'

'I'll discuss it with Dr Pierre but, please, don't be too hopeful. It's a big step for you to take, going out at night like that. It's going to be chilly after the sun goes down and it will be crowded and noisy and—'

'But you will take me if Pierre says yes, won't you?'

Caroline smiled. It was so difficult to deny Katie when she spoke in that wheedling voice. She had retained a childlike simplicity within her adult body.

'I'll do what I can.'

'Oh, thank you, thank you!'

Katie's childish cries were still echoing as Caroline went out through the door. Calling in to check on the children's ward, she found young Joseph, her leukaemia patient, sitting in the chair by his bed, reading a book. He was so absorbed that he didn't even notice she'd arrived, so she had time to glance at his charts. It appeared that the new medication she'd advocated was working wonders. Good!

She looked down fondly at the little eight-year-old. He was small for his age but that was to be expected. He'd had a tough time, medically. Leukaemia had been diagnosed when he was five and on two occasions he'd almost died. He'd been one of the first patients she'd cared for when she'd first arrived at the Clinique. She remembered the patience he'd shown as he waited for a bone-marrow transplant. Bernard, his elder brother, had been in hospital in Paris, undergoing tests to check out his suitability as a donor.

After the operation had been performed in Paris both brothers had come back to the Clinique to convalesce. Bernard had now gone home, but Joseph still required treatment and medication to ensure the success of the life-saving transplant.

'Caroline! I didn't know you were here.' The young boy looked up from his book and reached out a thin arm towards her. 'Bernard brought me this book when he came in to see me yesterday, but it's his new book and he wants it back today so I've got to keep reading.'

Caroline smiled. 'How are you feeling, Joseph?'

'Fine! When can I go home?'

'As soon as we can possibly get rid of you!' she said, affectionately ruffling his hair. 'I'll speak to Dr Pierre this morning about it.'

'About what?'

She drew in her breath as she heard Pierre's voice behind her. Turning round, she saw he'd changed into a light-coloured, summer-weight suit. His hair was still damp from the shower and he seemed to glow with good health.

'Joseph was asking when he could go home.' She handed Pierre the chart that she'd been studying. 'This new medication certainly seems to be working,' she added quietly.

Pierre nodded. 'You were right to suggest we change it. Well done!'

She smiled. 'Praise from the boss so early in the morning. I'm not sure I can take it.'

He grinned. 'Don't let it go to your head.' He leaned down to speak to their young patient. 'What's your book about, Joseph?'

'It's the history of aeroplanes. It's fantastic! Did you know that—' Joseph's eyes were shining with excitement as he described some of the aspects of the book to Pierre in great detail.

Caroline took the opportunity to go round the three remaining small patients. Out of the corner of her eye she could see Pierre sitting on the edge of Joseph's bed, discussing the book with him, seemingly as enthralled as the young boy himself. The arrival of the children's breakfast trolley reminded her that she ought to eat something herself if she was to get through the morning efficiently.

Leaving Pierre to carry on his conversation with Joseph, she went down to the small breakfast room. A couple of nurses were sitting in her favourite window-seat so she contented herself with the table by the door. The coffee in the cafetière was hot and strong and her croissant still warm from the *boulangerie* in the village. She knew that Mme Raymond collected them personally, and the baker would never be able to supply her with anything but the best!

As she finished and leaned back in her chair for a moment, Pierre came in, glancing casually around the room.

'I thought I might find you here. Katie says you're going to take her to the *son et lumière* tonight.'

He sank down onto the chair at the other side of her table. She noticed that his voice wasn't exactly stern but he certainly didn't seem pleased.

'I'm sorry, Pierre. I tried to discourage her but she's set her heart on going. What do you think of the idea?'

He frowned and stroked his chin from where the dark stubble had been shaved since his morning run. She held her breath, convinced he was about to tell her to stop sticking her neck out or some such similar reprimand, which had been quite customary in that far-off life when their child-adult relationship had been so different.

'It might do her some good,' he said, in a slow, thoughtful tone, 'but only if we both go with her.'

She felt a leaping of her spirits. It was purely a professional engagement but the thought of spending the evening with Pierre was exhilarating. Since their idyllic picnic at Le Touquet, when she'd obviously put him off the idea of further encounters, she'd longed for an opportunity to spend more time with him.

In the past two weeks she'd come to the conclusion that, whatever the future held, she had to make the most of the present as far as Pierre was concerned. When she got back to Hong Kong she didn't want to feel she'd missed out on the opportunity of the romance of a lifetime.

'I'd certainly feel safer if you were with me, Pierre. Katie can be a handful if she starts to behave like a spoiled child. We'd definitely better take her in her wheelchair. I know she's walking quite well now, but she gets tired and—'

'I certainly agree with you about the wheelchair.' He smiled. 'Besides, we'll know where she is all the time. I wouldn't want her to run away.'

'I doubt she'd do that. Her legs are very weak and…' Her voice trailed away, and she grinned as she saw the facetious expression on Pierre's face. He was winding her up in exactly the same way he'd done when she was a child.

'OK, I get the picture,' she said, beginning to rise. 'I'm going to get on with my clinic. The patients will soon be arriving and…'

He put a hand on her wrist to detain her. 'Sit down for a moment. There's plenty of time. Have another coffee.'

He picked up the cafetière and replenished her cup, before pouring some for himself. She sank down again and began to sip her coffee. Pierre was spreading apricot conserve on his croissant. He looked up at her, his eyes enigmatic.

'There's something I have to ask you.'

She swallowed hard, feeling butterflies swirling around in her tummy. The gentle tone of his voice told her that this had definitely nothing to do with their professional lives. She glanced around and was relieved to see that the nurses had gone and they were alone.

'Do you still want me to make that hotel reservation? I know that the last time we were out together it ended on a sour note so I've been careful not to push the matter. But if you think we could start where we left off before…' He paused, his eyes searching her face.

'Before I made my impossible suggestion about a financial partnership,' she said carefully.

He reached across the table and took hold of her hand.

'It was an impossible suggestion, Caroline. I'm glad you understand that it wouldn't work. But I thought you seemed decidedly cool towards me since we were at Le Touquet so—'

'Only because you seemed unapproachable,' she put in quickly.

He squeezed her hand, his fingers entwining with hers before he took his hand away as a young nurse came in.

'I didn't mean to be—unapproachable, I mean,' he said in a barely audible voice. 'Sometimes I'm simply preoccupied. I would have thought you understood me by now.'

'I do,' she said softly, feeling the gentle lift to her spirits that she'd so longed for since they were last together. Sitting here in her grandmaman's old sewing room, she felt a wonderfully warm closeness with Pierre. 'And in answer to your question...' Glancing around, she saw the nurse was now chatting to a colleague who'd just arrived. 'In answer to your question, I'd love to go to Normandy with you.'

His smile was boyish as he leaned forward across the table. 'How about next weekend? Jean was free last weekend and he's off duty tomorrow and Sunday so he won't mind if we take off together next Friday afternoon.'

'Friday afternoon? You mean two nights...and days, of course,' she added, trying desperately to prevent the pink flush from spreading over her cheeks.

He reached forward and touched her face with a gentle finger. 'You know, I thought you'd grown out of blushing. It used to be a sign that you were going to do something terribly mischievous.'

He removed his finger and she gave a sigh of relief as she saw that the two nurses were still involved in their own conversation.

'What about the wagging tongues when we load up your car?'

'What about them? Will it worry you?'

'No, of course not,' she said quickly.

She was going to behave like a woman of the world, as if romantic weekends *à deux* were all part of her normal life. She'd been propositioned numerous times, the first when she was seventeen, but she'd never wanted to take up any of the offers. But this wasn't a proposition. This was a coming-together with someone she'd always admired and now found she was falling in love with. She could feel her toes curling inside the sensible leather court shoes she always wore on clinic days.

She stood up, smoothing down her linen skirt to make sure she wasn't carrying any croissant crumbs with her into her consulting room.

'I need to go and check the case notes of my first patient,' she said quickly.

Pierre stood up and accompanied her to the door. 'So that's settled, then?'

'Yes, of course.'

'And tonight we'll leave soon after nine for the *son et lumière*. Wear something warm.'

His hand was resting lightly on her shoulder. She looked up at him, conscious that a man who was probably her first patient was just crossing the reception area. She had to pull her thoughts together and get into a working mood, and Pierre wasn't helping.

'See you later,' she said quickly, as she hurried across to her consulting room, closing the door behind her and leaning against it to compose herself.

Several deep breaths later she went over to her desk and picked up the folder from the top of the pile. Much of the medical data of the Clinique was computerised, but it was still necessary to keep track of letters from doctors and consultants with information about the patients they were referring.

All the patients she saw in her clinic had been referred by specialist consultants. Her role in the chain was to oversee the general welfare of patients who were being considered for admission to the Clinique. In the notes of her first patient she found the letter from his consultant, telling her that Gregoire Sebatier was twenty-nine and had been diagnosed as having multiple sclerosis.

Her eyes scanned the pages of notes before she picked up her intercom and asked the nurse at Reception to bring her patient in.

She greeted him at the door, holding out her hand in a welcoming gesture. He certainly didn't look like the image expected of someone suffering from a potentially crippling neurological disease.

'Monsieur Sebatier, do come in and make yourself comfortable.'

She noticed that his handshake was firm and that he held himself upright. He sat down without any stiffness and smiled across the desk at her.

'Call me Gregoire. It makes me feel younger.'

She smiled back. 'OK, Gregoire, would you like to tell me something about yourself?'

It transpired that Gregoire, after losing the feeling in one of his hands, had been given a brain scan a couple of years ago which had confirmed that he was suffering from multiple sclerosis.

'I was twenty-seven, Doctor, fond of sport, living life to the full, and it was like a bombshell.' He pulled a wry face. 'I thought wheelchair, crippling, all the things you see in TV medical dramas. I thought, that's my life over.'

Caroline stood up and moved round the desk so that she

could sit face to face with her patient. She could see that the young man was trying to put a brave face on his affliction.

'Multiple sclerosis is still an enigma, Gregoire,' she said gently. 'We don't know what triggers the disease and it affects each person differently. We can't cure it but we can control it with medication and specialised treatment. You've been seeing Jacques Mellanger, the neurological consultant who's recommended that you spend a few weeks here at the Clinique. Would you be happy to be admitted today? The sooner we start treatment, the better.'

Gregoire nodded. 'Anything you say, Doctor. I had a bad attack during the week. Couldn't feel my left side for a couple of days. It's still a bit numb and my eyesight's a bit dodgy but...' He paused and gestured with his right hand. 'I can still walk, talk and eat.'

Caroline leaned across and patted his hand. 'You've come to the right place. The cuisine in this place is excellent. I can't promise you a permanent cure but we'll try to improve the quality of your life. Now, I'm planning to start you on a drug you haven't taken before. It's called Avonex and it's one of the beta interferon range of drugs.'

Gregoire grinned. 'What's a beta interferon drug?'

Caroline smiled back. Gregoire seemed like the sort of intelligent patient who wanted to understand his own treatment. Some patients preferred to accept medication without knowing what it was they were taking, but she'd decided from the outset to be completely open with this personable young man.

'Beta interferon was initially developed as a treatment for cancer. Now it's being used for MS sufferers because it was discovered it decreases the number of attacks. We'll also give you some hydrotherapy treatment in the small pool we have hidden away in our underground health spa and you can go up to our specially equipped tower room and use some of the gymnastic machines designed to help tone up your muscles. I think you'll enjoy the experiences.'

It was good to see the sparkle return to her patient's eyes. He was young enough to respond to the drug she'd prescribed. It didn't work on older patients whose muscles had wasted away but with a formerly healthy person it could work wonders. And she was pleased she could make use of the small health spa that Pierre had created in the old cellars. It wasn't used nearly enough, in her opinion.

Soon after she'd arrived he'd given her the grand tour of the former cellar area. The old wine racks had been taken out and a small hydrotherapy area created, complete with plunge pool and the various jets of water necessary for the treatment. A qualified hydrotherapist was called in from Montreuil when treatment was prescribed.

She spent the next few minutes eliciting more information from Gregoire about his past medical history, his likes and dislikes and generally trying to make him feel at ease.

After she'd asked one of the nurses to take him up to his room on the first floor she settled down to study the case notes for her second patient, a twenty-year-old woman, expecting twins. That was one thing she liked about the work at the Clinique. She had such a varied workload—one moment she was considering neurology, the next she was plunged into obstetrics.

Madame Beatrice Rameau looked very small as she came in and crossed to the desk, apart from the large, round evidence of the twins which impeded her progress. Caroline could see that before the pregnancy she would have been very thin. Her arms in the cotton sundress looked positively emaciated and her matchstick legs looked barely able to support her extra weight.

'One of the first things we're going to do, Beatrice,' Caroline said, after she'd finished examining her patient on the couch, 'is fatten you up a bit.'

The young woman sat up and swung her legs over the edge of the couch. It was at that moment that Caroline heard the door opening and Pierre's voice telling her that he'd called in to pick up some case notes which had been wrongly delivered to her room.

'I'll be with you in a moment, Dr Chanel,' she called through the curtains that surrounded the couch. 'They must be on my desk somewhere. Help yourself.'

She could hear him riffling through her pile of notes as her patient started to query her last statement.

'How do you mean, fatten me up? I feel like an elephant.'

Caroline leaned across the couch towards her patient. 'Both you and the twins are underweight and this is one of the reasons that your obstetrician has suggested you spend the last few weeks of your pregnancy here. Now, if you'd like to get dressed and come out to see me, we'll discuss what we're going to do.'

She went out through the curtains to find Pierre sitting in her chair, holding the notes he'd been looking for.

He stood up and came towards her. 'I was waiting until you'd finished.'

'Why?'

'No reason. Is it a crime to want to see you in the middle of the morning?' Completely unexpectedly, he dropped a kiss on the end of her nose. 'Here, you can have your notes back.' He gave her a rakish grin. 'I thought you were alone so I had to make up some excuse.'

She laughed, feeling a bubbling up of excitement. 'What brought this on?'

He put a finger under her chin, tilting her face up towards him and then, gently, oh, so gently, he bent his head and brushed her lips with his. 'It was all that talk of our weekend away. I'm finding it hard to concentrate and the sun's shining in through the windows, reminding me that the summer will soon be over and—'

'Dr Bennett, I'm dressed now…'

Caroline pulled herself away from this most unprofessional encounter as her patient came out through the curtains.

'Dr Chanel, how nice to see you again.' Beatrice Rameau was smiling as she extended her bony hand. Turning to Caroline, she said, 'Dr Chanel was so kind last year when I lost my first baby.' There was a catch in her breathy voice. 'I don't know what I would have done without him. I'm so afraid for the babies I'm carrying. I can't help thinking that—'

'We're not going to lose these twins, Beatrice,' Pierre said softly. 'Your first baby was malformed and wouldn't have survived so nature took its course. The twins you're carrying are normal and healthy according to the results of your scans but, as I heard Dr Bennett saying just now, you'll have to go on a healthy diet to increase their weight. Have you been keeping to the diet I suggested to keep yourself healthy?'

Beatrice blustered at first, but the truth came out after a few attempts to pull the wool over Pierre's eyes.

'I told you to stick to the diet, Beatrice, for your own good,' Pierre said quietly. 'You were too thin. You'll have to build up your strength while you're waiting for the birth. We'll also have to monitor your blood pressure pretty closely because that was one of the problems last time.'

Beatrice nodded. 'I'll do everything you say this time, Doctor,' she said.

Caroline glanced at Pierre but his expression gave nothing away. Reading between the lines, she gathered that Beatrice had not been the most perfect patient when she'd been pregnant last time. This was the sort of information that rarely found its way into the case notes. Pierre would, no doubt, tell her about the problems later.

As the sky began to darken outside her window, the air in her little room began to take on a decided chill. Checking through the clothes she'd brought with her from Hong Kong, she chose the one and only warm trouser suit. It rarely saw the light of day out in Hong Kong—only in the middle of December or January did she wear it—but here, at the end of July in France, it would definitely be necessary at midnight if not before.

Katie was waiting for her in a state of avid expectancy. Helene had helped her dress in warm trousers, ankle-length boots and a couple of sweaters. She took hold of Caroline's arm and allowed herself to be eased into the wheelchair.

'Anyone would think I couldn't walk,' she was muttering under her breath, loud enough for Caroline to hear and maybe take pity on her.

'You're too big to be carried if you get tired,' Caroline said, in the sort of tone she might have used with a child. She was feeling decidedly weary at the end of her day and would have preferred to curl up in her room with a good book.

Katie glanced up at her doctor and seemed to take the hint that her patience was not to be stretched too much this evening. Folding her hands in front of her over the rug that the nurse was neatly tucking in over her knees, she said in her sweetest voice, 'It's very kind of you to take me out, Caroline.'

The door opened and Pierre walked in, looking as fresh as he had done first thing that morning. The combination

of Pierre's arrival and Katie's obvious attempt to stop being querulous did wonders for Caroline's mood. She could
feel her spirits lifting and her weariness evaporating.

'Are we all ready?' Pierre asked. 'Is your mother not
coming with us, Katie?'

'I phoned her but she had a prior engagement,' Katie
said. 'A dinner party or something she couldn't cancel. I
forgot to tell you.'

Pierre frowned. 'That means we've got a spare ticket
because I reserved four over the phone this morning.
Maybe…'

'Why don't we ask Gregoire if he'd like to go with us?'
Caroline said. 'I was speaking to him in his room about
half an hour ago and he seemed rather down. It's not much
fun sitting around on your own on a Friday night.'

Pierre smiled. 'Good idea, Caroline. Will you go along
and suggest it?'

'I'll bring him out to the car if he wants to come.'

'Well, what are we waiting for?' Pierre took hold of the
back of Katie's chair and began wheeling it towards the
door.

Gregoire was delighted with the idea of an evening out,
and on Caroline's advice put on a warm sweater. Pierre
had decided they would have to take the Renault Espace
which was always used when several patients needed
transportation at the same time. With the wheelchair
stowed in the boot and Gregoire and Katie sitting in the
back, Caroline climbed in beside Pierre.

The spectacle of the *son et lumière* was due to take place
in the grounds of the citadelle at Montreuil. The ancient
ramparts of the castle looked impressive in the twilight as
Caroline walked beside Pierre, who was pushing Katie's
wheelchair.

Gregoire, she noticed, had one hand on the back of the

seat as well. She had already formed the opinion that having Gregoire with them had been an excellent idea. Katie was positively blossoming under the unexpected pleasure of chatting to a young man.

Gregoire, for his part, seemed to find Katie fascinating, and the two patients exchanged stories about their various problems. In the car, Katie had been bemoaning the fact that she couldn't remember anything about her former life, and Gregoire had told her jokingly that it might be a good thing. He'd said there were lots of mistakes he'd made in the past that he wished he could forget.

'Having a fresh start must be fantastic!' Gregoire had told Katie. Her reaction to this had been to roar with laughter and say that she'd never thought of it like that.

Now, as the four of them eased their way through the large crowds towards the seating area, Caroline glanced up at Pierre.

'I think this could be beneficial to both of them,' she whispered, under cover of the surrounding noise and the non-stop chatter of their patients.

He smiled down at her and nodded. 'What a wise young woman you are today. All these brilliant ideas and decisions.'

'I'm glad the boss approves.'

'Don't know what I'll do without you.'

She swallowed hard. The dream would have to end some time. She would leave all this and go back to her former life—wouldn't she? Was there any way she could prolong this temporary idyll?

How would Pierre react if she told him she was losing interest in being independent? With his outlook on life he was unlikely to encourage her changing ideas. No, it was enough for him that they were to have a romantic fling, possibly a mere weekend away together, before they resumed their previous lifestyles.

So she'd better keep her thoughts to herself and enjoy each day as it came.

Pierre had reserved seats in the front row so that they could accommodate Katie's wheelchair. Gregoire sat down on the seat next to Katie, which meant that Caroline and Pierre were able to sit together at the other side.

As the sun sank and the sky darkened, the lights of the grassy, partially wooded area where the spectacle was to be staged were turned on. The trees took on a magical aura as lanterns swung from their branches; carefully concealed lights illuminated the grassy banks and the small hillock leading up to the ramparts. Caroline found it quite breathtaking when the stirring music started.

The *son et lumière* spectacle was based on the story of *Les Misérables* by Victor Hugo which had been inspired by his visit to Montreuil during the last century. The scenes enacted by some of the adults and children of Montreuil brought a glimpse of life in a bygone era. Caroline found it poignantly stirring; reality and fiction were intertwined as the players portrayed their ancestors and some of the fictional characters in Victor Hugo's novel.

She was utterly enthralled during the entire performance and as the final explosion of fireworks lit up the midnight sky she found herself clapping and cheering enthusiastically with the rest of the audience.

'Wasn't that fantastic?' Katie's eyes were shining in the light of the firework illuminations. 'Did you enjoy it, Gregoire?'

Caroline saw her patient put his hand over Katie's and smile down at her. 'Can't remember having such a good evening for ages. Of course, the company helped.'

Katie giggled. Pierre touched Caroline's arm. 'Shall we stop off for a coffee in the square?'

Caroline smiled. 'Love to! If our patients aren't too tired.'

Gregoire laughed. 'The night is young. And I'm not working tomorrow.'

Pierre chose a table outside a small café near the fountains so that they could watch the iridescent colours of the cascading water while they sipped their coffee. Looking out across the cobbled square, Caroline could feel the carnival atmosphere that prevailed. Couples strolled hand in hand in the moonlight, young families were being hustled away to bed amid laughter and merriment.

Pierre squeezed her hand under the table. 'Better get our patients back to the Clinique.'

'Oh, they don't seem to be coming to any harm,' Caroline said, glancing across the table at their charges.

Gregoire was holding the sides of Katie's wheelchair, leaning forward towards her and telling her an obviously fascinating story.

'You didn't!' Katie was squealing in amusement.

'I did!'

There was some discussion about whether they should go back, but Pierre insisted.

Arriving back at the Clinique, Katie said she wasn't tired. Gregoire said he could stay up all night A firm night sister met them at the main door and took immediate charge of their patients.

'Thanks, Caroline,' Katie called over her shoulder as she was wheeled away.

'It's been great.' Gregoire said, putting a proprietorial hand on the back of Katie's chair.

'How about a nightcap?' Pierre said quietly, as soon as their patients had been spirited away.

Caroline stood in the open doorway, half-turned towards the moonlit garden. Like Gregoire, she felt as if she wanted to stay up all night. The weariness she'd felt at the end of her working day had completely vanished.

'Lovely!'

Glancing up at Pierre, she thought she saw an expression of surprise in his eyes. He'd probably expected her to decline.

He took her hand as he closed the main door and led her across the gravel forecourt towards his rooms. She stood back as he fished for his keys and opened the heavy oak door. It swung open with a creaking sound.

'Keep meaning to get an oilcan and sort those ancient hinges out,' he said.

As she stepped inside Pierre's domain she had the distinct impression he was nervous. It was almost as if, because he hadn't expected her to accept his invitation, he now didn't know how to handle the situation. Strange, when they'd known each other for so long! But it was all about adaptation, seeing each other in a completely new light. How long would it take before they felt completely at ease in each other's company?

She breathed in that indefinably welcoming odour that permeated old houses.

'That's such a friendly scent,' she said, sinking down into the corner of the sofa. 'The château used to smell like this in Grand-mère's day. It's a combination of ghosts and centuries of people living their lives to the full. You've taken away the old smell from the château and replaced it with a clinical odour that's completely devoid of anything welcoming—I'm not making a criticism, simply stating a fact,' she added quickly.

He laughed as if relieved that she'd broken the tension. 'You always did have the strangest ideas, Caroline. So, what would you like to drink? There's a bottle of champagne in the fridge if—'

'Oh, yes, please! So you were expecting a midnight visitor after all!'

'Can't believe my luck!'

He disappeared into the kitchen, returning with a bottle and two long-stemmed glasses. She lay back against the cushions, feeling like the cat that was about to lick the cream. It wasn't the thought of champagne which was intoxicating her but the prospect of becoming closer to Pierre.

They clinked their glasses together. Pierre put the bottle on the small table next to the sofa and eased himself down on the cushions beside her. She took a long sip and then another, causing the tingly effervescence to play havoc with her already heightened senses. She realised that the way she was looking at him from under her long lashes was probably most provocative to a virile, athletic man like Pierre.

Moments later he was removing her glass, setting it down on the table and pulling her gently against him. She sighed with happiness as she put her arms around his neck, drawing his head down towards hers.

His kiss was tenderly caressing. She moulded herself against him, revelling in the contact of their bodies. Impatiently, he tugged at his shirt, pulling it up over his head. And then his fingers were deftly undoing her blouse, searching inside for the warm, sensually aroused breasts that were straining against him, waiting for his caressing hands to tantalise them.

'Stay here with me tonight, Caroline,' he whispered against her hair.

And at that moment the full reality of what was happening between them hit her like an icy blast. She didn't want to creep out in the morning like a fugitive with something to hide. She didn't want to risk the sniggers of the night staff as she made her way back to her own room. The love she felt for Pierre was a precious and beautiful sentiment which they should consummate somewhere far away from the prying eyes of their colleagues.

Gently, she detached herself and ran her hands over her tousled hair. She saw the worried expression in Pierre's eyes and leaned across to touch the side of his cheek as she tried to explain how she felt.

'I'd love to stay but I don't want the first time to be…in a compromising situation. Next week, far away from patients and colleagues, we can just be ourselves. Believe me, Pierre…'

He put a finger against her lips. 'I understand. That was why I was surprised when you came back with me tonight. Because you must have known how any kind of contact would have ended.'

He pulled himself to the other side of the sofa and gave her a rakish grin. 'I only have to look at you now to… Oh, Caroline, go to bed quickly before I stop being such a nobly motivated…'

He was standing now, walking over to the door. 'Come and give me a chaste goodnight kiss and then vanish quickly, you wicked temptress.'

She laughed at his impression of an anguished lover, his hand over his heart, feigning heartache. As he kissed her goodnight, she whispered, 'Have you made the reservation at the hotel for next week?'

He pretended to look surprised. 'So, it's still on, is it?'

'I certainly hope so.'

A shaft of light from his door illuminated her path across the forecourt to the front door. The night nurse at the desk looked up briefly and smiled, before resuming her paperwork.

As she ran up the stairs to her room she was beginning to wonder if maybe she'd been too cautious in turning down Pierre's suggestion that she stay the night. If she'd followed her instinct she would have been in his arms now and…

No, she wanted to savour that first moment of real commitment. What was she contemplating? Commitment? Neither of them wanted commitment from the other, did they? That was one of the things they had in common—a desire for independence. The only thing she should be contemplating was a short-term romantic fling.

That was what the small voice of reason was trying to tell her, but her heart was directing her otherwise. She realised with a pang that she wanted the whole works. Pierre to herself for the rest of her life. What price independence when it involved ignoring the love she was feeling for him?

As she laid her head down on her pillow, she reflected that Pierre had made it perfectly clear what he wanted— and it wasn't commitment.

## CHAPTER SEVEN

CAROLINE woke very early on the day that she and Pierre were to drive down to Normandy. The night before, as she'd lain in bed, with the moonlight streaming in through the open curtains, she'd felt as she had when she was a child, waiting for Christmas morning to dawn with its promise of presents and treats.

She sat up in bed and stretched her arms up towards the white-painted ceiling that sloped away towards the dormer window overlooking the garden. Through the open windows she could hear the excited chattering of the house martins under the eaves. The tingling feeling of anticipation under her skin was doing nothing towards making her into the sort of rational human being required to deal with her patients. For their sakes alone, she'd better pull herself together.

Standing under the shower, she deliberately turned on the cold tap and gave a shriek as the icy water cascaded upon her. At least, it delivered a shock to her senses and brought her out of the semi-comotose state in which she'd spent the last few minutes when all her thoughts had been about Pierre. Since she'd drunk her glass of champagne with him a week ago and they'd been on the brink of making love, she'd tried to pretend to herself that she was ready for a light-hearted affair with him.

But she knew she wasn't! She'd admitted to herself that this wasn't what she wanted but she'd go along with it if that was all that was on offer.

And it is all that's on offer, she told herself firmly as

she ran down the steps to the first floor. So hold yourself back emotionally or you'll get hurt when it's time to go back to Hong Kong.

Easier said that done, she reflected as she opened the door to Katie's room. Her patient was not alone. Gregoire was sitting beside her on the padded window-seat, leaning towards her in animated conversation. Caroline felt a pang of alarm. Pierre had suggested they monitor the situation very closely. Having brought these two patients together, they had to consider the consequences if a full-blown romance developed between them.

Gregoire's multiple sclerosis wasn't going to go away. They were holding it back with the help of drugs and treatment but his future was still uncertain. And Katie was still very much like a child in many respects. She had a long way to go before she could lead anything like a normal life.

Caroline put on her bright, professional smile. 'You're an early visitor, Gregoire. Couldn't you sleep?'

He smiled back. 'Katie was the one who couldn't sleep. So I came along to keep her company.'

'Gregoire came along to cheer me up, Caroline. I gave him an early morning call and invited him to breakfast.'

The door opened and Katie looked up expectantly. 'Ah, here's our breakfast. You can put it down on this table, Helene.'

Why had she the feeling that Katie was beginning to treat this place like a hotel? Caroline held her tongue but decided she'd have to check with Pierre to see if he approved. And how would Mrs Smith react if she knew her daughter was becoming fond of one of the other patients?

Fond was too weak a description. Besotted was more like the real truth!

Well, it takes one to know one, said the small voice of

reason inside her head. Maybe she was recognising her own emotions in Katie. But the poor girl couldn't possibly be in the same dilemma in which she found herself. At least Katie seemed to know her own mind.

Leaving her two patients to enjoy their breakfasts, she went along to Beatrice Rameau's room. The prospective mother of twins was sitting up in bed, spreading butter on a croissant.

'Everything OK, Beatrice?'

Beatrice smiled. 'Fine thanks, Doctor. Is it this morning I have my weekly examination?'

'It is indeed, but I'll come back later,' Caroline said.

Was it her imagination or did Beatrice look slightly plumper in the face? Certainly, she'd lost that gaunt, peaky look she'd had when she'd been admitted last week. Caroline made a mental note to get the full case history from Pierre. He'd been promising he would explain the situation but they'd never got around to having a conference about it. Perhaps today they could find a few minutes.

But the day proved even busier than usual because they were working against time to get everything finished during the morning so that they could set off for Normandy immediately after lunch.

As they finally loaded the bags into Pierre's car, Caroline was still in full working mode and finding it difficult to believe that they were really going to be off duty for a full weekend. Jean came out to the car with them, carrying Caroline's heavy holdall. She'd intended to travel light but at the last moment she'd panicked herself into packing extra garments she probably wouldn't wear…but might!

Pierre glanced up from the open boot and grabbed the holdall from Jean. 'What happened to the kitchen sink, Caroline? I could always put it on a roof rack.'

Ignoring Pierre's jibes, she looked up at Jean. 'Are you sure you're going to be OK, Jean? I've written instructions about Gregoire's treatment on his chart. The hydrotherapist will come in this afternoon and—'

'Caroline, you've already explained all this,' Jean said. 'Now, go off and enjoy yourself. The Clinique is quiet this weekend and we're not admitting again until Monday so stop worrying. And I've got Giselle to help me this afternoon and Pierre's father arrives from Paris this evening so—'

'Your father's coming here?' She turned to look at Pierre.

He slammed shut the lid of the boot. 'Didn't I tell you? Must have slipped my mind. He actually offered his services. I think he's getting bored in retirement. He misses the buzz of hospital life. It's the same with Giselle. She doesn't know what to do with herself away from the Clinique.'

Caroline was pleased that Giselle, the doctor she'd replaced for her maternity leave, had been able to put in a few hours. She was a frequent visitor to the Clinique on some pretext or other. Now in the final weeks of her pregnancy, she'd confided to Caroline that she felt as fit as a horse and was bored to tears with the waiting. She'd already told Pierre that she wouldn't mind working a few hours to pass away the time and had jumped at the chance of an afternoon session.

She'd also told Caroline that she couldn't wait to get back to work full time. Her mother was going to look after the baby when it was born. It had made Caroline realise, with a pang of dismay, that her own departure from the Clinique was growing nearer with every day that passed. She mustn't waste a moment of her precious time.

As they drove out through the wrought-iron gates she

glanced back at the tall, impressive building. The sun was shining on the tower and she felt a lump rising in her throat. For far too long she'd fantasised about owning it and now there was another dream to add to the fantasy.

She would be over the moon if she could combine the two—if she could be mistress of the château and lifelong companion to Pierre. Leaning back in her seat, she gave an involuntary sigh.

'Is that a sigh of weariness or relief to be getting away?' Pierre asked as he drove carefully past the turning that led to the village.

A group of children was standing beside the road, laughing and joking with each other, looking terribly vulnerable to the traffic that threatened the peaceful rural scene. One step from the narrow causeway and a child would be hurt. Occasionally, they had to deal with minor accidents along the road, children falling from bicycles or narrowly escaping something worse. The traffic had been much lighter when Caroline had been here as a child, and she felt it was only a matter of time before something major would disrupt this close-knit community.

'It's a sigh of anticipation,' she said boldly, and was rewarded by Pierre's hand covering hers with a significant squeeze.

'Good! I'm feeling the same way myself.'

'Well, before we become total and utter pleasure-seekers I've got to ask you about Beatrice,' she said quickly. 'I did the weekly exam this morning. Her scan was fine. Both babies still underweight, but Beatrice has put on a kilo.'

'A whole kilo—wow! She must be taking this pregnancy seriously after all.'

They were driving up to the *péage*, the control area at the beginning of the *autoroute*. Pierre slowed down to take a ticket from the machine before they drove onto the wide road. Caroline waited until they were through the barrier before saying,

'You told me that the last pregnancy was difficult. Would you care to elaborate?'

She heard the sharp intake of his breath and saw his knuckles whiten as he gripped the wheel.

'The last pregnancy was an unmitigated disaster. It should never have happened. Beatrice was totally unprepared…but let me start at the beginning. During her teenage years, Beatrice was into drugs. Having kicked that habit, she became anorexic. Several times she was on the point of death but we pulled her back.'

'So, she was treated here at the Clinique?'

Pierre nodded, his eyes still on the wide, undulating sweep of the *autoroute* as it carved its way through the beautiful countryside. Cows still browsed peacefully in the meadows beyond the busy road. Gulls swooped overhead, occasionally winging their way downwards to catch the warm current of a passing car.

'Two years ago, she was still being treated here for anorexia. We thought we'd cured her. Then last year she came in late in her pregnancy and there was nothing we could do. She'd been smoking heavily and was a virtual alcoholic so the baby had already died in the uterus.'

'How awful! But what about her husband? He seems such a nice man when he comes to visit her.'

'Oh, she wasn't married when she was pregnant last year. She was in a relationship with an undesirable character who's not around any more, thank goodness. Her husband is a sensible young man who, I'm hoping, will be a good influence.'

'So Beatrice got married after her disastrous pregnancy last year, did she?'

'Yes, they got married a few months ago and he seems

absolutely perfect for her. Well, that's what her parents told me and I hope they're right. Beatrice has been such a difficult daughter. They've given her everything she wanted—well, everything that money could buy. I think that was half the problem. She got spoiled rotten as a child and couldn't break out of the mould.'

'Why couldn't I find any of this in the notes?'

'Because I prefer not to have these things written down. I pass on information to valued colleagues and—'

'So I'm a valued colleague, am I? Not just a temporary—'

'Yes, you are a valued colleague,' he said quickly. 'And don't mention the word "temporary" because it reminds me how little time we have left together.'

She drew in her breath. Dared she tell him how her ideas had changed? How she couldn't bear to imagine life without him? She looked across at his handsome profile and felt her heart turning over. Surely he must be feeling as she did? Surely he couldn't ignore the chemistry they had between them, the looks they gave each other across the room in the Clinique when a patient was talking to them and they both suddenly took off into a world of their own?

Well, at least she did! What Pierre was thinking she had no idea. She'd better leave it until the end of the weekend when she might be able to pluck up courage to tackle the subject.

They reached their hotel in the Suisse Normand towards the end of the afternoon. Stepping out of the car in front of the attractive-looking building with its dormer windows open invitingly in the sunshine, curtains blowing in the breeze, Caroline smiled across at Pierre.

'What a lovely hotel! "*Au site Normand*",' she read on the sign at the front. 'So you've been here before?'

'Lots of times. The people who own the hotel are now very dear friends of mine.'

And indeed, Mme Feuvrier, the owner of the hotel, certainly seemed pleased to see Pierre. A charming lady, wearing a becoming summer dress swirling around her legs, she welcomed them in the cosy bar-reception area as she chatted to Pierre, before handing him a key.

'You didn't sign in or anything,' she said to Pierre as they crossed a pleasant courtyard at the back of the hotel.

He smiled. 'It's like coming home here. Very relaxed. Beats all those huge, impersonal hotels. The personal touch, that's what you get here. And the food…!'

He put his fingers to his mouth as he smacked his lips.

Caroline laughed. 'That's a very Gallic gesture. The English don't get so excited about food.'

'That's because they don't know how to cook proper food. Here in France…'

'Careful, I'm half English, remember!'

'The strange, unpredictable half.' He put an arm around her shoulder and drew her against him as they went into a charming old building across the courtyard. It looked as if it might have been converted from an ancient stable block but the restoration work had been sympathetically accomplished in keeping with the general ambience.

Opening the door to their room, Pierre stood back to allow her to go in first. 'So, what do you think?'

'It's absolutely charming!'

She crossed the thick rose-coloured carpet to reach the open casement windows that overlooked the courtyard. The cretonne curtains, tied back from the window with gold tassels, had picked up the rose colour of the carpet, scattered with small blue flowers. She hardly dared to glance towards the wide double bed which seemed to dominate the room. The quilted cover matched the curtains to perfection. Hidden beneath she knew there would be crisp sheets where, tonight, she would lie in Pierre's arms.

She shivered and turned back to look out of the window.

'You're not cold, are you?' He crossed the room to put both hands on either side of her arms as he looked quizzically down at her. 'You're not having second thoughts, are you? Regretting coming away with me?'

She smiled up at him, revelling in the tender touch of his fingers on her bare arms. 'Of course not.' She was about to say that she was a big girl now but realised that would bring on a predictable response.

'I think I'd like to get some fresh air before…before supper.'

'I was about to suggest it,' he said lightly. 'I'll take you down to the river and we can have a drink at one of the riverside cafés.'

He took her hand as they walked up the ancient cobbled street that wound its way to the end of the little town. The path to the river sloped steeply down between high hedgerows where the late afternoon sun glinted on the leaves. Boats were skimming the surface of the water, happy holidaymakers laughing and talking as they cruised along.

Pierre chose a small café beside the river and led the way onto a wooden platform that jutted out over the river. They sat down at a table nearest to the water. Caroline leaned over the wooden fence at the side of the platform and dipped her hand in the river.

'I love the feel of cold, cold river water. It makes me think I'm on holiday.'

'You are,' he told her as he leaned across the table to take hold of her hand. 'For two whole days.'

She leaned back against the chair and closed her eyes, allowing the warmth of the sun to bathe her eyelids. It was like a dream. Here she was with Pierre all to herself, no work to do, no worries…well, nothing she couldn't handle when she got back to the Clinique.

A young waiter set a glass of kir, the drink that was made up of *crème de cassis* and white wine, in front of her and she opened her eyes.

'Happy holiday!' Pierre said, raising his own glass.

She clinked her glass against his and took a deep refreshing drink. 'Mmm, I love the taste of kir. I never drink it anywhere else but in France. I wouldn't dream of ordering one in Hong Kong.'

His eyes flickered. 'Don't you miss the sophistication, the shopping, the night life, the—?'

'No! Not at all. Look, let's not talk about Hong Kong when we're in this beautiful place.' She looked out across the river at the reflection of the trees, which rippled with every passing boat. If only this could go on forever…

'Pierre…'

'Yes?'

She swallowed hard as she wondered whether this was the moment to tell him how she felt. To say… But what could she say that wouldn't frighten him away from her? He'd made it quite clear he didn't want a financial partnership or any other kind of partnership that would spoil his independence. He was waiting for her question. Quickly, she improvised. It wasn't difficult because she'd been contemplating broaching the subject all the way down in the car.

'Where do the staff at the Clinique think we're going this weekend?'

He smiled. 'I knew something was worrying you. I don't know where they think we're going and I don't care—do you?'

'Not really. But Jean knows where we are, doesn't he?'

'Of course. And he entirely approves—as does my father.'

Her eyes widened. 'You told your father you were coming away with me?'

'Oh, I didn't say I was taking the difficult, fractious child from next door…'

She pulled a face at him and he grinned boyishly. '…I simply said I was having a weekend away with a special friend.'

She felt herself relaxing. If she couldn't be anything else she would enjoy being Pierre's special friend. 'So what made your father want to come along from Paris for the weekend?'

'I told you he was an orthopaedic consultant before he retired, didn't I?'

She nodded. 'And he's getting bored in retirement, I gather. But what about your mother?'

'She's still working in paediatrics. Mum's ten years younger than Dad so until she retires he's on his own for long hours. He's offered his services before but I've never taken him up on it.'

'Why not? I would have thought it would be a perfect arrangement.'

He looked surprised as she voiced her opinion. 'To be honest,' he said slowly, 'I wanted to make a go of the Clinique before I called him in. He was very sceptical when I first discussed my idea of buying the château. I wanted to prove…well, to prove that I had a viable proposition because he tried to dissuade me.'

'Ah, I see.' What she saw, reading between the lines, was that Pierre and his father had had an important difference of opinion and now there was an attempt at reconciliation.

'Another drink, Caroline?'

'Oh, no, thanks. It's going to be a long evening, I expect, so I'd better pace myself. Don't want to get squiffy.'

He laughed. 'Yes, I don't want you falling asleep…in the middle of your supper.'

She stood up and leaned over the wooden fence that guarded the platform. A couple of white swans were gliding gracefully past, the sun glinting on their bright orange beaks. They seemed to be looking up at her with haughty disdain as they pursued their uncomplicated lives on the river.

'Let's go back to the hotel,' she said quietly. 'I'd like a bath before supper.'

She had a sudden vision of the bathroom that adjoined their bedroom—the long, wide bath with scented soap and sachets of bath foam and shampoo had looked so inviting when she'd first peeped in. Now she felt suddenly shy at the idea of sharing a bathroom with Pierre.

But she needn't have worried because back at the hotel Pierre chose to sit in the window-seat, studying the newspaper he'd bought at the paper shop. When she disappeared into the bathroom he remained motionless by the window, apparently totally absorbed by an article in *Le Figaro*. As she soaked away the cares of the day she found her excitement mounting.

It felt strange to be walking across the courtyard and into the bar-reception area again with the handsome stranger beside her. Because that was what he seemed like, even though she'd known him for many years. Something had changed in his bearing as he'd put on the immaculate jacket and well-pressed trousers. She'd chosen to wear her ivory linen dress together with the silver necklace that had belonged to her grandmother.

Pierre had complimented her on her appearance as he'd

watched her putting the final touches to her toilette as she'd sat at the small dressing-table by the window.

'I remember that necklace,' he'd told her softly, as he'd stood behind her.

She'd looked at his reflection in the mirror and had felt a surge of love welling up inside her. All the years she'd known him had led her to that moment. The necklace, which he'd seen around her grandmother's throat, had seemed to symbolise the continuity of their friendship. It couldn't possibly have ended like that...could it? Before it had even had time to blossom into something more tangible and permanent?

He'd bent to fasten the clasp and, before raising his head, had put his lips against her bare skin. She'd felt a tingle of happiness diffusing through her whole body.

Now, as they walked together into the bar-reception area, Caroline walked tall, holding her head high, feeling proud of the man beside her and revelling in the promise of the evening to come.

Pierre led her to a comfortable armchair beside the wide, open fireplace. The logs which had been placed in readiness for the cooler weather to come were concealed by a huge vase of flowers, irises and roses intermingled with wild ferns. Pierre ordered champagne and while she waited for the ice bucket to be positioned she watched in fascination as the tropical fish in the nearby aquarium swam in colourful groups, pausing to stare out of the glass with lugubrious expressions.

'I'm glad those fish aren't edible,' she said. 'In Hong Kong, when I go to a restaurant where the clients can chose their fish live from the tank, I can never bring myself to select one. I always end up having the vegetarian dish.'

Pierre laughed as he handed her a glass of champagne. 'Well, don't eat vegetarian tonight because the meat and fish in this hotel are out of this world. Mme Feuvrier's husband and son are the cooks and they're absolutely first class.'

Indeed, she couldn't quibble with Pierre's prediction as she sailed through all the courses of the dinner. Starting with an *amuse-bouche*, which was a nibble of mouth-watering home-made pastry with asparagus, they continued with fresh salmon in a superb secret-recipe sauce. Then there was a slight pause—to aid the digestion, Pierre said—while they ate a fascinating concoction, *spécialité* of the region, known as a *trou normand*.

'It literally means a Normandy hole,' Pierre said, as he spooned up the icy sorbet which had been liberally doused in Calvados, the special Normandy liqueur distilled from apples.

'It's fabulous. Definitely cleanses the palate and makes you anticipate the next course.' Caroline, looking out of the window, saw that the sun was sinking behind the roof-tops. This meal was the perfect end to her day—or rather the beginning of her night. There were hours and hours of pleasure ahead of her.

She had chosen pheasant to follow her fish course. This had been cooked in another secret-recipe sauce which tasted of apples, Calvados and cream. It seemed that the chef of the house had his own excellent repertoire. After the main course, a selection of local cheeses was presented on a large platter, followed by a salad, again designed to cleanse the palate.

'Dessert?' Pierre asked her.

She smiled. 'Something very small. I'd no idea I could eat so many courses at one sitting.'

She chose a tiny *crème caramel* before they retired to their corner by the fireplace for coffee and Calvados.

'I can honestly say that was one of the best meals I've

ever had,' she said as she leaned back in her chair. And one of the most interesting in terms of conversation, she thought but didn't say out loud. They'd talked about a wide range of subjects. She hadn't realised how knowledgeable Pierre was on matters of interest to both of them. It would take a lifetime before they ran out of topics of conversation.

If only a lifetime were possible! Well, she'd take as much as she had time for before it was time to call a halt. But looking across at Pierre as he raised his glass to his lips, she knew without a doubt that she would never be able to go back to Hong Kong. She couldn't possible go halfway round the world and put all those miles between them. There had to be another way out.

She would stay on in Europe, get another job in a hospital. Somewhere within striking distance of Montreuil so that she could keep up a friendship on an occasional basis. But she would have to be subtle so that Pierre didn't suspect what she was up to. A hospital in Paris would be a good idea…or London. She could travel through the tunnel and—

'You're looking very serious all of a sudden.'

Pierre's words interrupted her revolutionary thoughts. 'Am I?' She smiled. 'Just making plans about the future.'

His eyes flickered. 'Care to share them with me?'

'Not yet, but you'll be the first to know when I've finalised the details.'

For some moments he was silent, his expressive eyes searching her face for some clue as to what she was planning, but he didn't pry any further.

Draining his glass, he stood up and held out his hand towards her. 'A quick walk around the town square and then we'll turn in.'

She knew he was putting off the moment when they

would be really alone. She felt a tremor of excitement as he put his arm around her and escorted her out through the door of the hotel. She nestled against his side, revelling in the warm masculine smell of him with the heady overtones of his distinctive aftershave.

They stood in front of the small fountain in the middle of the town square. The moon above shone a pale light that mingled with the illuminated spheres surrounding the cascading water. Neither of them spoke. Caroline felt that the moment seemed to encapsulate her happiness at being with Pierre.

She felt his arm tighten around her waist as he led her back to the hotel, through the courtyard and up to their room. As he closed the door he leaned against it and took her into his arms. She sighed as she pressed herself against him, feeling the throbbing pulse of his love drawing her into an ecstatic web where the world ceased to exist and only the present moment had any reality…

Hours later, as she lay sated with the excitement of their love-making, she couldn't remember how she'd somehow been transported to this island of the senses which was their now very crumpled bed. She laid her head in the crook of Pierre's arm and he stirred in his sleep, automatically drawing her closer to his side. She listened to the rhythm of his breathing.

Looking up at the ceiling, barely distinguishable by the light of the moon that streamed in through the window, she reflected that she'd guessed it would be something like this when she and Pierre finally consummated their love. But she hadn't known to what extent her feelings would be stretched. Nothing in her previous experience of life had prepared her for the sheer ecstatic bliss that she'd known as Pierre had taken her to a higher plane, some-where between cloud nine and over the moon.

Gently, she disentangled herself from Pierre. If she tried to sleep in his arms she would find her senses rousing again. And she needed to pace herself because tomorrow was another day and she needed to gather her strength!

In the morning, they climbed the steep hill that led to the take-off point for hang-gliders. Caroline watched, fasci-nated, as a couple of men literally flung themselves off the end of the launching pad and sailed away on the breeze, like giant birds. Looking down at the vast panorama with the Orne river snaking its way through the valley, she breathed in the fresh air as she tried to remain calm and rational about their weekend together.

That's all it was—a weekend they'd managed to fit into their busy lives. There would be other weekends—pro-vided she was subtle and didn't scare him away with her scheming. If she was careful she could handle the situation. It required a certain amount of sophistication which she doubted she possessed at the moment but she could en-deavour to find.

She would be Pierre's part-time mistress, someone so unobtrusive that he wouldn't realise the self-styled position she'd assumed. And this would be totally satisfac-tory...wouldn't it?

Glancing up at him now as his eyes scanned the im-pressive scenery, she knew it wouldn't be at all satisfac-tory. She would always want more—more than Pierre would be prepared to give. Wouldn't it perhaps be easier and less heartache if she went back to Hong Kong and tried to forget him?

# CHAPTER EIGHT

THE idyllic weekend had passed far too quickly. As they turned off the *autoroute* at the Montreuil exit Caroline began to feel the shades of the prison closing in again. She was locked in a battle with herself over how she was going to handle the new emotions that were churning away inside her.

Glancing at Pierre's handsome profile as he steered the car through the barrier, she felt a pang of deep anxiety. Their love-making had been, by turn, turbulent and exhausting, tender and provocative, but always deeply satisfying. Her emotions had never been so charged, and so fulfilled. As she'd lain in Pierre's arms on the second night, drenched in perspiration, her skin tingling with the promise of more hours of sensual gratification, she'd known she was at a crossroads.

Never again could she go back to her complacent way of life, where all she'd yearned for had been fulfilment in her chosen career and the occasional holiday or weekend away in some exotic location. Pierre had shown her what life was all about—love, with a capital L! All sorts of trite but true phrases were going through her head as they drove past the turning to the village. No man was an island—very true, but try telling that to Pierre!

'Are you ready to meet my father?' Pierre asked casually, as he drove in through the open wrought-iron gates.

At that late hour on a Sunday evening at the end of an idyllic but exhausting weekend, all she wanted to do was escape to the undemanding solitude of her room and reassess what she planned to do with the rest of her life.

'Will he be expecting to meet me?'

'I don't see how we can avoid it. I did tell him that he used to know you years ago.'

'Did I meet him when I was a child?'

'I think you probably met him a couple of times when he came over to see his brother, my uncle. He used to like to roll up his sleeves and play at being a farmer—for a few hours before he remembered he had a pressing engagement in Paris.'

'I don't remember him,' she said, as she climbed out of the car and stretched her cramped limbs. The air outside the car was surprisingly warm after the air-conditioning. A heat haze had formed around the sinking sun, giving the garden a feeling of ethereal unreality.

It was good to be back, even though their weekend together had brought up more problems than it had solved. How was she to behave towards him now that they were lovers? Did he want her to cover up the situation?

It certainly didn't seem like it as he shepherded her through the door, one arm loosely placed on her shoulder. She did a double take as the tall man standing in the reception area came towards her. This was Pierre in another twenty to thirty years, tall, distinguished, thick hair grey at the temples, high, aristocratic cheek-bones crisscrossed with living lines and a wide, welcoming smile on his still strikingly handsome face.

She was surprised she didn't remember him but, then, as a child you weren't interested in the tall grown-ups who were leading their own lives and getting on with their work. Unless they made a special effort to amuse you, they simply merged in with the scenery.

'Pierre! Introduce me to your lovely friend.'

She took the outstretched hand and smiled up into the face of Pierre's father. He'd certainly been an eye-catcher—still was, in spite of his indeterminate age. Was it possible he was in his sixties? He looked ageless. If she was still in contact with Pierre at this age then this was how he would look.

'You remember Caroline, the little girl whose grand-mother used to tire of her so easily and—'

'Now, Pierre, that's not fair,' Dr Chanel senior put in with a wry grin, before looking down at Caroline and asking, 'Does he tease you like this all the time, my dear, like he did when you were a child?'

She laughed. 'Constantly!'

'But are you really the little scallywag who—? Oops, sorry, now I'm doing it! But you must be exhausted after your journey. I've persuaded Mme Raymond to prepare a little cold supper in Pierre's rooms so that we can escape the clinical atmosphere of this place. Come along and I'll give you a quick medical report over a glass of wine.'

'I wouldn't mind doing a quick round of the patients before—'

'No point, my boy,' his father put in airily. 'It's as quiet as the grave. I've just been round and checked everybody. The nursing staff will alert us if there's anything unto-ward—which is unlikely. And Jean is prowling around somewhere. A good doctor, that young man.'

'So, did you enjoy living in my little domain, Dad?' Pierre asked, as soon as the three of them were ensconced in his cosy sitting room.

Both men were sitting on the sofa, their glasses of wine held by their stems with long, tapering fingers in exactly the same manner, both eyeing her across the hearthrug as she snuggled against the soft cushions of the armchair.

'I found it most comfortable. A little cramped after the

large rooms I'm used to in Paris, but perfectly adequate for a bachelor.'

It was the way the older man dwelt on the word 'bachelor' that alerted Caroline once more to the fact that there had been quite a sizeable rift between Pierre and his father. Moments later, some of the mystery evaporated as she heard Dr Chanel senior asking, 'How's that awful ex-wife of yours?'

'Doesn't improve with age,' Pierre said with a wry grin. 'But she's a necessary evil.'

'Such a pity you married her.' The older man turned to fix an enquiring look on Caroline. 'What do you make of the dreaded Monique?'

Out of the blue like that, the question threw her completely. 'Well, I've only seen her a few times and she was always in a hurry, Dr Chanel, so—'

'Do call me Christophe, my dear. Yes, that's Monique for you. Always in a hurry when it suits her. I warned Pierre against her right from the start and—'

'Dad, it's no use raking up the past,' Pierre said quickly. 'Now, how about that cold supper I found in the kitchen?'

Caroline wasn't in the least bit hungry but she went through the motions of toying with the cold roast ham and the green salad which the cook had so kindly prepared. As they ate their supper, Christophe Chanel gave them a blow-by-blow account of the events of the weekend in the Clinique. There hadn't been any emergencies and it appeared that the patients had been left in expert hands.

'So, will you come again if I need you, Dad?' Pierre said, as he carefully poured boiling water onto the coffee-grounds of the cafetière.

Caroline saw the delighted look on the older man's face before he deliberately disguised it with a more sophisticated expression.

'Well, I could come along if you had a staffing problem, yes. I'd have to check what your mother's up to, of course, but—'

'Yes, of course. What is Mother up to this weekend?'

'She was taking a paediatric clinic on Saturday and to-day she was planning to catch up on all the little chores that mount up during the week. You know what women are like, don't you? She also needed to wash her hair and so on. I think, to be honest, she was glad to get me out of the way.'

Pierre opened his eyes in a wide, innocent stare. 'Oh, I can't believe that, Dad.'

Both men laughed. Caroline stood up. 'If you two will excuse me, I'll go up to my room. I've got a lot to sort out before the morning—including washing my hair,' she added with a wry smile.

The two doctors Chanel stood up. 'You must be tired after your journey, my dear,' the older man said. 'I hope to see you in the morning before I leave for Paris.'

Caroline said she hoped so too. Pierre walked with her to the door and opened it. As she was about to pass through he leaned towards her and kissed her tenderly on the lips.

'Thank you for a wonderful weekend,' he whispered in that husky tone that sent shivers running down her spine.

She met his gaze with unblinking eyes. How could he be so loving and not be disturbed by his emotions? Did he imagine their relationship was going to stand still? Couldn't he see that it had to blossom further or die? He couldn't have his cake and eat it!

But even as the hard thoughts ran through her mind she knew there was nothing she could do about the situation. Pierre was Pierre and she couldn't change him—even if she wanted to. Perhaps his intransigence was one of the facets of his strong character which had attracted her to him. She turned away and crossed the forecourt.

As she walked across the reception area the nurse on duty looked up and smiled at her.

'Did you have a good weekend, Dr Bennett?'

'Fabulous!' she surprised herself by saying. The cat was out of the bag now. She had nothing to hide. She was linked to Pierre in some indeterminate way and she found she was proud of it. How could anyone be ashamed of the wonderful experiences she'd shared with Pierre?

Her head held high, she climbed the stairs. As soon as she could she would contact David in Hong Kong and ask him to make a permanent replacement. Perhaps the temporary doctor who'd taken her place might be suitable. And then she would make plans for a working career somewhere in France or England. Somewhere accessible to this little piece of heaven where she would return from time to time, giving the impression that she was happy with the sophisticated, worldly relationship she shared with Pierre.

He would be free to keep his precious independence and she would be able to live her life to the full without him for most of the time. It was a big compromise but it was the only way out of the dilemma.

David was surprised to hear her voice when she phoned him next morning. It was late afternoon in Hong Kong and she could tell from the buzz of voices in the background that he was in his busy office, dealing with staff and patients who were waiting to see him.

'What a pleasant surprise, Caroline! I thought you'd disappeared off the face of the earth. Not even a postcard!'

'Sorry, David, but I've been busy.'

She heard the rustle of paper as he signed something and gave instructions to somebody to bring him another cup of coffee. Smiling to herself, she could visualise the view across the island of Hong Kong, the harbour busy with boats, and behind the nursing home the towering mass of the Peak. She'd been happy there but that was a chapter of her life that was now closed. She was ready to move on.

She took a deep breath. 'I'd like to be released from my contract, David. I've decided to stay on in Europe and—'

'So you've met Mr Right?'

'Stop fishing!' How astute could you get! 'This is a professional decision. I'm giving you time to find a replacement and I sincerely hope there won't be a problem with that, David, because—'

'Don't worry about it, Caroline. The young doctor who's replaced you in a temporary position is shaping up nicely—in more ways than one, I might add. I took her out to dinner a few times—just to get to know her—and she's a delightful girl.' He gave a little chuckle.

Caroline smiled. David didn't change. 'Well, I'm glad it's all working out. Your temporary doctor will be happy to take a permanent post, I take it?'

'She'll be over the moon!'

'Well, I'm glad I've made somebody happy.'

'I'll miss you, Caroline. We all will. When you've got your love life sorted out, come out for a holiday. Bring the boyfriend with you.'

'I'll be needing references, David,' she hurried on, trying to think of all the practicalities she needed to take care of, 'because I'm going to apply for another job in Paris or London. This post is definitely temporary here.'

'No problem, Caroline. I'll send you a glowing testimony and anything else you require. Good luck!'

The phone went dead. She stared into the receiver, hoping that no one else in the Clinique had picked up an extension. Especially not Pierre! She would tell him her plans in her own good time. Meanwhile, she had to keep up the pretence that she was going back to Hong Kong. She'd think of a reason to stay in Europe when she'd finalised a new job.

A new job! Glancing round her little room up here among the eaves of the château, she wondered if she would ever find anything as congenial as this situation. This was like working from home! No hassles with apartments or rented rooms. Perhaps when she'd settled the job situation she would buy herself a permanent apartment or small house. She could afford it with her legacy.

Yes, that would be her consolation for losing out on the château—and being unable to gain a permanent hold on the other prize in her life.

Downstairs, on the first floor, she began her morning rounds. Katie was happily eating breakfast—alone for once.

'Mum came in yesterday afternoon. She wanted to have a word with you but I said you'd gone away for the weekend. She's coming in again this afternoon.'

'Good. I'll come in and see her then.'

Caroline felt a pang of apprehension. Mrs Smith had probably got wind of the budding romance between her daughter and Gregoire. Well, they hadn't been breaking any of the Clinique rules—so far! But it seemed only a matter of time. She made a mental note to enlist Pierre's help this afternoon.

Beatrice was already out of bed, her breakfast tray waiting to be collected. Caroline glanced over it. 'You've eaten every crumb. Good girl!'

Beatrice smiled. 'The twins have been kicking like mad so I decided they were hungry and reminding me I'm eating for three.' She looked across at Caroline. 'Are you going to be around when my twins are ready to be delivered?'

'I certainly hope so. Why?'

Her patient drew in her breath. 'I'd like you to help Dr Chanel with the delivery,' she said shyly. 'I think you two make such a good team. You seem to know what the other one's thinking without words. And this time I don't want anything to happen to my babies.'

Caroline leaned forward and squeezed her patient's hand. 'Nothing is going to happen to your babies, Beatrice. Provided of course, that you keep up your healthy regime. Are you sleeping well?'

'Like a log!'

'And taking all your vitamins?'

Beatrice grinned. 'I positively rattle.'

Caroline smiled. 'I'll be back to see you later.' As she went out onto the landing she reflected that it was true what Beatrice had said about her and Pierre being a good team. They did work well together—now! There had been a lot of tension when she'd first arrived but all that was behind them.

They'd sorted out their professional relationship. Why couldn't the personal situation run as smoothly? Maybe Pierre thought it did! This was all he needed from her. A light-hearted romance. No commitment, no long-term plans or—

She stopped short in her ruminations as she saw Pierre coming out of the children's ward. He came towards her with that easygoing, fluid movement of the hips that made her knees go weak. Putting out both arms, he placed his hands against her arms and drew her towards him.

She glanced around, but they were quite alone. 'Sleep well?' he asked gently.

She nodded, the feel of his hands on her arms unnerving

her. 'Did you?' This was such a trite conversation, masking more important questions!

'I kept on dreaming about this beautiful woman who vanished every time I tried to take her in my arms,' he said softly. 'What do you think the dream psychologists would make of that?'

She moved backwards so that there was a sizeable space between them as she heard one of the doors opening. Janine, the paediatric sister passed them, her eyes studiously on the ground.

'I've no idea,' Caroline said in reply to Pierre's cryptic question. 'Perhaps you're reaching for the unobtainable. That would seem logical but it doesn't make sense.'

'No, it doesn't. Because I seem to have everything I want.'

She looked up into the enigmatic eyes. 'Are you sure?'

His eyes flickered. 'There are some things I'd change if—'

He broke off and she waited with bated breath. 'If what, Pierre?'

A couple of nurses came round the corner, chattering and laughing. Pierre became the professional doctor again, squaring his shoulders and telling Caroline they'd discuss the situation later.

As she went into the children's ward she knew the moment had passed and maybe it would never return. But then again…was it possible that Pierre was changing?

How could she show him that it wasn't enough to love in a temporary situation? That two people who felt for each other as they did would sooner or later have to make a permanent commitment.

In the children's ward she found Joseph, her leukaemia patient, in high spirits.

'Dr Chanel says I can go home tomorrow. Maman is

going to take me to Disneyland at the weekend and Grandmaman is going to buy me a new bike.'

Caroline ruffled his hair and smiled. A little spoiling was what this dear little chap needed to put behind him the rigours of his earlier life.

'That's because you've been such a good boy and done exactly what we asked you to do. I've got to take one last blood sample from you, Joseph so...'

'No problem!' The little boy grinned as he rolled up his sleeve.

Caroline carefully selected a vein that hadn't been used too often. Joseph's arm resembled a pincushion but he never complained. Deftly, she inserted the needle and withdrew the required amount of blood, placing it in the sterile container which she would take down to the small laboratory for analysis.

Downstairs, after visiting the lab, she was paged by Reception. 'A message for you, Dr Bennett,' the nurse at the desk told her.

It was a hand-written note, inviting her to breakfast in Pierre's rooms, but it had been signed by Christophe. How quaintly old-fashioned to send her a note! Pierre's father could have telephoned but instead he'd chosen the time-honoured way of getting his message across. She glanced at her watch. She mustn't stay long, but then she remembered that Dr Chanel senior would be wanting to get back to Paris so he wouldn't have much time to spare.

'Come in, my dear, and let's close the door before that son of mine spots what I'm up to.'

She smiled as Christophe closed the door behind her and ushered her into the small kitchen where the delicious smell of coffee tantalised her nostrils.

'And what are you up to, Doctor—I mean, Christophe?'

He reached for the coffee-pot. 'How do you take your coffee, my dear?'

'Black,' she said, waiting as patiently as she could to hear more about why this meeting had to be so clandestine.

'I want you to talk some sense into that son of mine.' The dark hazel eyes searching her face were unnervingly like the younger pair she was so used to.

She took a sip of her coffee. 'In connection with what, exactly? And before you go on, I really don't think I have any power over the way your son thinks.'

'Oh, but I think you have, Caroline. I've never known him so content.'

'Content? That's not a word I'd ever use to describe Pierre. He's restless, always wanting to move on and—'

'You're right, but I think he could be tamed.'

'I wouldn't want to be the one to tame him, as you say,' she said carefully. Just what was the older man getting at?

'It's the financial arrangements of this place I'm talking about. He's still tied up with that ex-wife of his and I feel it's my fault.'

'Your fault? But why?'

He pushed a plate of warm croissants across the table towards her but she shook her head. 'No, thank you.' Absently, she began to peel an apple as she listened to what Christophe had to tell her.

'When Pierre first brought up the idea of buying the château I thought he was mad. I didn't think it would work. To finance the purchase he was going to use the money left to him by his uncle—my brother—and also a legacy from my father over which I had the power to sanction or not.'

She narrowed her eyes in deep concentration as she looked across at the earnest expression on Christophe's face as he continued his explanation.

'My father was also a doctor. He was also very much a philanthropist—rather like Pierre, I suppose. He put a clause in his will which stated that if Pierre wanted to use the money in a viable medical proposition he could do so—provided I approved.'

'And you didn't approve,' Caroline said softly, putting down the knife and placing a piece of apple in her mouth.

Christophe nodded. 'I didn't approve and so, because of the wording of the will, the money had to stay in a trust fund which would be used to finance a medical project of my choosing. So far it has remained untouched. But now…'

He spread his hands out in front of him on the kitchen table. 'When I see what a success my son has made of this place I want to help him—but he's so stubborn. I broached the subject last night, told him I'd sanction the money but…'

The kitchen door was opening. She hadn't heard the outer door creak because she'd been so wrapped up in Christophe's story. Pierre stood on the threshold, his face an enigmatic mask.

'What a cosy domestic scene! I didn't know you were holding a breakfast meeting, Dad.'

'It's not a meeting—it's a social occasion,' Dr Chanel senior said quickly.

Pierre gave his father a wry grin. 'I couldn't help over-hearing you saying something about sanctioning the money, Dad. As I said last night, I'd prefer to keep the situation as it is.'

Christophe frowned. 'Even if it means you have to keep on the partnership with your ex-wife?'

'The financial partnership, yes. Legally, I can't buy her out when it suits me. She helped me when there was no other money forthcoming,' Pierre said. 'I had no choice then but to make her a financial partner in the château. I can't wriggle out of that one.'

Christophe's brow was deeply furrowed. Caroline looked from one man to the other. The younger one whom she loved now with all her heart in spite of his stubborn character and the older, possibly wiser but equally vulnerable man whom she was beginning to regard with real affection.

'There must be a way out,' Caroline said quietly.

Both men stared at her for a few seconds in silence. Pierre was the first to speak. 'If you can come up with one then—'

'Why not ask Monique outright if—?'

'No!' Pierre put a hand on her arm. 'I'm not going to go crawling to that woman, begging her to—'

'Maybe you won't have to beg!' At that precise moment Caroline felt like shaking Pierre! Why couldn't he climb down from his high horse and make contact with Monique? She could only say no, but that would hurt his precious pride. Unless, of course, he was still carrying a candle for his ex-wife.

As soon as the treacherous thought entered her mind she tried to dismiss it. Pierre couldn't have given out as much love as he'd given her over their idyllic weekend and still retain some of his former affection for his wife…could he?

The older man stood up, flinging his linen napkin down on the table, which presumably indicated that his patience was exhausted. But when he spoke his voice was perfectly controlled. 'I must be getting back to Paris. Your mother worries until I actually arrive. She's not working today so we've got tickets for the opera tonight.' He turned to look at Caroline. 'Goodbye, my dear. So nice to meet you again.'

They waved goodbye to Christophe as he drove round

the corner of the Clinique towards the gates. As he disappeared from sight, Pierre turned back to look at Caroline.

'I think the old man likes you.'

'The feeling's mutual,' she said quietly.

He took hold of her hand, his eyes searching her face. 'You do see I can't get rid of Monique, don't you?'

She took a deep breath. 'I see that you're too stubborn for your own good. Just because your father wouldn't help you out five years ago is no reason for holding out now. You're cutting off your nose to spite your face.'

She waited for his reply, worrying that perhaps this time she'd gone too far. She'd spoken out of turn and probably frightened him into thinking he'd made a mistake in allowing them to become lovers, with all the rights that intimacy gave. She'd dared to challenge his precious independence and she'd have to face the consequences.

He was looking at her as if he'd never seen her before. 'Who would have thought that young, innocent girl would grow up to be such a spirited, outspoken creature?' he said.

She turned away and walked quickly towards the main door. She would immerse herself in her work. Somehow she would get rid of the frustration that was gnawing away inside her.

'Legally, my hands are tied,' she heard him call after her, but she kept on walking.

# CHAPTER NINE

SITTING in her consulting room, watching the September leaves drifting across the lawn, Caroline reflected that there had definitely been a strained atmosphere between herself and Pierre since their idyllic weekend in Normandy. She realised that she'd gone beyond the bounds of mere friendship when she'd spoken out about his financial arrangement with Monique. And she guessed that one of the things that Pierre couldn't stand was a bossy woman!

She sighed as she turned back to check through the case notes on her desk. There was a full ten minutes before the first patient was due but she liked to be in control of the situation before the work started. She picked up the first file from the top of the stack but her mind continued to dwell on Pierre. He must have thought he'd prefer to have Monique lecturing him about finance than herself!

Why hadn't she just kept quiet? Well, she reasoned that she was more anxious to get rid of Monique than Pierre was! Monique's physical presence around the Clinique always annoyed her.

She looked up, startled, as the door opened. She hadn't yet done her homework.

'Good morning, Caroline. Sorry to startle you. I did knock but you couldn't have heard.'

Caroline gave a sigh of relief as she saw Giselle, the doctor she was temporarily replacing. During the time she'd been at the Clinique she'd warmed to this down-to-earth and experienced doctor. With her long golden hair fixed to the top of her head, she was of striking appearance, even with the extra weight that her pregnancy had brought to the usually slim figure.

'I was on my way down to the shops and I thought I'd call in to see if you needed any help.'

Caroline smiled. 'Come and sit down. It must be tiring, carrying that bump around with you.'

Giselle sank into a chair. 'It is, but you'll find out for yourself one day.'

Caroline pulled a wry face. 'Maybe—if I find the right man.'

'I thought you had.' Giselle's face was wreathed in smiles. 'I thought there would be a proposal in the offing when you and Pierre went down to Normandy. I mean, anyone with any sense can see that you're made for each other.'

'Pierre's not the marrying kind,' Caroline said quickly.

'He was once.'

'That's the trouble. He's been bitten once so he's not going to risk it again.'

'Oh, that's what they all say. My Thomas was exactly the same. His first wife took him to the cleaners when they divorced but I managed to convince him that all women aren't cast in the same mould. And then I threw away the Pill and got pregnant, which clinched the matter because Thomas had always wanted children.'

Caroline shrugged. 'Mine would have to be a virgin birth. Since Normandy we've been just good friends—and sometimes not even friendly.' She found it easy to confide in Giselle because she knew their conversation wouldn't go further than these four walls.

'Oh, dear, I don't like the sound of that, but I'm sure there must be a solution.'

Giselle, optimistic as ever, didn't know the half of it!

But she was good to have around the place and she would be pleased if Caroline found something to occupy her time.

'Would you like to stay and do some filing for me? There's a pile of case notes in the examination cubicle that needs to be put away in the cabinet. You're the only person I could trust to get it right.'

Giselle's face lit up at the prospect. 'I love this little consulting room,' she said as she hauled herself out of the chair. 'Can't wait to get back here after the baby's born— Oh, sorry, Caroline, didn't mean to sound as if I'm pushing you off. Well, if you're not going to marry Pierre, what are you going to do? Go back to Hong Kong?'

Caroline could hear Giselle stacking papers through in the small cubicle as she made a final attempt to bone up on her first patient.

'It's all in the air at the moment,' she said vaguely. 'I'll let you know when things are more settled.'

As she applied herself to the first page of notes she found herself wondering when that would be! She'd made enquiries at medical agencies in Paris and in London and started checking the ads for appointments in the magazines that were delivered to the staff common room, but nothing had appealed to her yet.

'When I've finished this filing I'll tidy out these cupboards, Caroline,' Giselle called. 'I meant to do it before I went off on my maternity leave but I never got around to it.'

'Well, don't do too much. You've only got a couple of weeks to go, haven't you?'

'Something like that, but I'm as strong as a horse,' she replied reassuringly.

There was a tap on the door and a nurse ushered in the first patient. Caroline put on her bright, professional smile and gave her full attention to the case in hand, pleased that as she concentrated on the welfare of the patient her own problems receded.

Shortly before lunchtime she realised that Giselle was still busily clearing out cupboards as if her life depended upon it. Something in her fanatical demeanour triggered a warning bell. Was this a case of the nesting instinct that came upon humans and animals alike as their time approached?

'You're sure you're OK, Giselle?' Caroline asked anxiously, as the last patient of the morning disappeared through the door.

'I'm absolutely fine,' she answered. 'My back aches a bit but that's only to be expected and—Ooh!'

Caroline was into the cubicle before Giselle's long-drawn-out cry had finished. 'I think you'd better lie down, Giselle,' she said firmly, as she saw the anguished look on her colleague's face.

'It's nothing, it's only a little twinge.'

Caroline heard the door to her consulting room open and close again as she was helping Giselle to lie down on the examination couch. Pierre's face was a study in perplexity as he poked his head round the curtains.

'What's going on?'

'Caroline's practising her bedside manner,' Giselle quipped before her face creased up in pain again. 'I was clearing out one of my cupboards when my backache turned to…I think it's turned into a contraction.'

She stared up at Caroline, as if pleading for moral support. 'I think it would have come on even if I hadn't been cleaning out cupboards, don't you, Caroline?'

Caroline tried to smile, but her face felt frozen. Why on earth had she allowed Giselle to indulge in all this physical activity? She bent down and placed experienced hands over Giselle's abdomen.

Giselle was a doctor so Caroline didn't feel entirely to blame for allowing the frenzy of physical activity that morning. She should have known the score herself.

Caroline glanced up at Pierre to see how he was taking this. To her relief he seemed to be accepting the situation as normal.

'Pregnancy does strange things to women,' he said, his face creased in a philosophical smile. 'I expect you were preparing your nest this morning.'

Caroline smiled. 'That's what I was thinking.'

'One of us should check if there's any widening of the cervix,' Pierre said, taking charge of the unusual situation.

'Caroline can check me out,' Giselle said quickly. 'I expect it's only a warning twinge but—Ooh…'

Caroline's examination of the birth canal revealed that it was dilating rapidly.

'I think it would be easier all round if we delivered you here,' she said as she raised her head. 'We've got all the equipment and it looks as if you're one of these people who has precipitous births—very little warning before a sudden onset.'

She'd barely finished speaking before amniotic fluid flowed over her hand as Giselle's waters broke over the examination couch. Pierre came in and started swabbing the area down in preparation for the delivery, donning a mask and gown and helping Caroline into hers.

By this time Giselle had lost some of her rationality and was clinging to Caroline's hand. She emerged from her temporary lapse of good humour to say that she'd prefer to be a doctor than a patient.

'Won't be long,' Caroline said quickly. 'I can see the head.'

'I know it's a girl because I saw her on my last scan. Has she got my hair?'

Caroline smiled. 'I can't tell at this stage and I think we'll need to wash it when she emerges. Are you sure you don't want anything to help you with the pain of the contractions?'

'No, thanks. I'm checking out just how much I can take. I wanted a natural birth and you can't get more natural than this. How far on am I?'

'You can push again now, Giselle, because I've eased out the shoulders... There she is!' Pierre said, as he placed the slippery baby in Giselle's arms. 'And, yes, when she's been cleaned up I think she'll have your hair.'

Caroline looked at Pierre. He was pulling down his green mask and as their eyes met she saw the expression of tenderness that always moved her.

She turned away to take charge of the newborn infant, running through all the routine checks while Pierre expelled the afterbirth and settled Giselle comfortably against some pillows.

'And now, Dr Giselle, I think we'll take you up to Obstetrics and surprise everybody,' he said with a boyish grin. 'Some people will do anything to spend more time at this place.'

Giselle laughed. 'I honestly had no idea this was going to happen when I came in this morning. I'd been awake with backache in the night but that was all.'

'Never under-estimate backache in a pregnant woman,' Pierre said.

'It's different when you're the patient,' Giselle said, as Caroline helped her into a wheelchair.

Caroline realised that it was way past lunchtime and she was decidedly hungry, but she didn't want to leave Giselle until she was firmly settled in Obstetrics. Pierre had excused himself already, saying that he had some business to attend to. As she crossed the reception area, pushing the wheelchair, on her way to the lift she saw the unmistakable figure of Monique hunched over some papers at the desk. Pierre, beside her, was gesticulating about something.

She turned away and gave all her concentration to Giselle. Going up in the lift, she was surprised to hear Giselle say, 'Did you see Monique just now?'

'Couldn't miss her, but I expected you to be too wrapped up in your gorgeous daughter to notice.'

'I can always smell a rat at fifty paces.'

Caroline laughed. 'Sounds like you dislike her as much as I do.'

'She's only stringing Pierre along, you know. She's got a new boyfriend and she's trying for every penny she can get. He's years younger than her and no money to speak of so Monique is trying to make a profit out of her share in the château. He visits her in her cottage in the village.'

'Does Pierre know about this boyfriend?'

'I doubt it. Why should he?'

They had reached the door to Obstetrics and the nursing staff were about to take over. Caroline promised to return after lunch and check again on mother and baby.

As she went back down the staircase to the first floor she couldn't help thinking that this boyfriend could be the answer to her problems.

# CHAPTER TEN

CAROLINE couldn't believe her eyes when she looked out of the landing window on the last day of September. Gregoire and Pierre were running down the path through the garden, both sweating as if they'd done a few miles in spite of the fact that it was still very early in the morning. Gregoire's treatment for his multiple sclerosis was obviously working!

She continued hurriedly down the stairs to the ground floor reception area so she was just in time to witness the two men coming in through the main entrance.

'I don't believe it!' she said, clapping her hands together in sheer delight. 'Is this really you, Gregoire?'

The young man grinned as Pierre put a hand on his shoulder, smiling his approval.

'Gregoire is making remarkable progress. It's early days but I'm quietly confident we're holding back the symptoms. With the drugs and treatment he's now taking, he'll able to carry on a normal life for a long time to come.'

Gregoire was panting heavily, but looking remarkably fit as he echoed Pierre's sentiments. 'I know the score. I'll never be fully cured but life's going to be pretty good during the times when we're controlling the MS. Thanks a lot for taking me out with you, today, Dr Chanel.'

Pierre smiled. 'I don't know who took who. I had difficulty keeping up with you at first.'

He was already moving away, back towards the main door. 'I'll have to work hard to keep up the pace with him,' he said, as he looked back over his shoulder at

Caroline. 'Dr Bennett, could you come over to my place for a few minutes? I won't keep you long because I know you're busy.'

Caroline glanced at the nurse on the reception desk, knowing that Pierre's professional manner had been entirely for her ears. She followed Pierre out of the main door.

'I need a shower first but I thought we could have breakfast together on our own,' he said, as he tried to resume his normal breathing after the exertions of the run. 'Not often we get chance to be alone.'

'And whose fault is that?' she said quietly, as Pierre unlocked his door to allow it to creak back on its hinges. 'I've had the distinct impression you've been avoiding me, except on duty.'

She heard the sharp intake of his breath and realised she was sticking her neck out again. Well, too bad! It was time she stopped playing the dutiful little woman and gave him a few home truths. Their relationship couldn't go on like this. See-sawing of emotions was OK if you were sure of each other's affections—and she'd felt very insecure during the past few weeks.

'Look, let me take this shower and then we'll talk, Caroline. I've been thinking about us—about our relationship—and, yes, I have been avoiding you because I didn't like the way you took sides with my father against me.'

He was running up the stairs now but he leaned over the bannisters to watch her reaction.

She looked up at him and noticed the way his hands clenched the wooden rail in a defiant manner.

'That's called sulking,' she said lightly, a wry grin on her face.

He pulled a face at her. 'No, I was simply making the point that I didn't want to be told what to do.'

'And you thought I was bossing you around, didn't you?'

He laughed. 'Well, you said it!' He turned to continue on his way to the bathroom. 'I need this shower before I drip any more sweat on the floor. Could you start the coffee, Caroline?'

She could, but was she going to? As she walked into the little kitchen she was toying with the idea of having a sulk herself! That would teach him to take her for granted!… No, it wouldn't. It would just drive him further away—and she wanted him to return to the closeness they'd experienced before she'd become—as Pierre had put it—so bossy.

But how could she put her point of view across? How did you get your own way with a stubborn man? She realised she had a lot to learn and no one to guide her. For an instant, as she spooned coffee into the cafetière she felt as if her grandmother was watching over her.

Grand-mère would have known what to do and would have advised her. She'd had to cope with a difficult man and had chosen to go it alone in the end. Pierre was difficult but he was worth the effort. And he was an honourable man—not like her grandfather, who hadn't known right from wrong.

Listening to Pierre now, as the strains of his deep voice in the shower wafted down from the floor above, intermingled with the sound of the cascading water, she knew this was the man she wanted to spend the rest of her life with. There would be fights, there would be tears, there would be all the rich drama of life. But there would also be love—if she didn't blow her chance!

'Compromise is what's needed,' she announced as Pierre came to the kitchen a few minutes later.

She pushed the plunger down on the cafetière with a

vicious movement that caused it to overflow. Pierre stopped rubbing the towel over his tousled hair and reached for a cloth.

'Here, let me do it.' He started to mop up the spill from the table.

He was very close to her now. The combined scents of soap and aftershave mingled with the spilled coffee and suddenly she couldn't hold her emotions in any longer.

'Pierre, I—'

'Darling, what is it?' His long, comforting arms were around her. She snuggled her head against the soft towelling of his dressing-gown, revelling in the masculine aroma that mingled with the other scents. He was all man, all desirable muscular man, but with all the complicated emotional tangles that went with loving someone so infuriating!

She raised her head to look at him. 'I don't know if I can go on like this.'

His brow furrowed. 'What do you mean?'

'When we were together in Normandy I thought we had something special. But then we came back and—'

'But, darling, we can't live on cloud nine all our lives.'

She loved the expression in his eyes as he looked down at her, his lips so close.

'I don't want to live on cloud nine. But I do want to know where I stand.'

Oh, dear, would he take this as an ultimatum? Perhaps it was. It was make-or-break time.

'At this moment in time you're standing on my foot,' he said, his voice huskily tender. 'But I'm not complaining because you're as light as a feather and it brings your face nearer to mine.'

'Oh, Pierre, you're avoiding the issue!'

'Am I?' he whispered as he bent his head and kissed

her on the lips. She gave an involuntary sigh as his kiss deepened. He pulled her closer, so close that she could feel the beating of his heart through the soft material of his robe.

'Caroline, you don't know how I've missed you,' he said throatily, his mouth hovering closely against hers. 'I needed time to think about where we were going together.'

'And what did you decide?' she said quietly.

His reply was to scoop her up in his arms and carry her towards the stairs. 'I decided, like you, that we had something very precious between us, something worth keeping at all costs.'

She twined her arms around his neck as he carried her up the stairs. He pushed open the door to his bedroom, placing her gently on the white quilt. Her hands still entwined around his neck, she looked up at him with pleading eyes.

'At least we agree that our relationship is special, Pierre. But will it last?'

For answer he swooped down, gathering her in his arms, and as his caresses roused her senses to ecstatic heights she lost all thoughts of the future. Only the present moment counted. As their bodies fused in exquisite mutual desire she heard him whisper, 'I love you, Caroline.' And she knew that was all that mattered.

Coming back to reality at the end of their love-making, she snuggled against him, remembering his whispered words of love as the climactic sensual waves still tingled under her skin.

As long as Pierre loved her she could deal with any problem that might arise.

He stirred on the bed beside her, drawing her close against him.

'How about breakfast?' she said, looking up at him. 'I'm

starving. I was hungry before you hijacked me in Reception and now I could eat a horse.'

He laughed. 'Ever the practical one! Shall I cook you one of your English breakfasts?'

'With scrambled eggs, toast, mushrooms and...' She paused as she disentangled herself to sit on the edge of the bed. 'Have you got all those things?'

'No, but I can get them in the village in the time it takes you to mop up the coffee— Sorry, I mean make the coffee!'

She aimed a pillow at his head. He ducked and reached out his arms towards her. But she was already making her way into the bathroom.

As she climbed into the wide, ancient bath, she felt a tingle of happiness running down her spine. It was going to be all right between them. They hadn't solved any of the practicalities but the main ingredient of their relationship was intact. They loved each other. What could go wrong?

She banished the worrying twinge that threatened to undermine her newfound optimism. Love would always find a way—wouldn't it? She realised she was being naïve but that was the way she was made. All her thoughts of a sophisticated relationship were pie in the sky! She could no more handle the thought of being Pierre's mistress than she could work out the practicalities.

Not to mention sitting on an emotional see-saw for the rest of her life! That wasn't what she wanted. But she would have to tread warily so as not to scare him off.

Down in the kitchen she had time to make fresh coffee before Pierre returned from the village with his packages.

'Eggs, bacon, mushrooms, fresh baguettes, peaches—I couldn't resist these luscious peaches. Have one while you're waiting for me to produce this gourmet breakfast.'

She sank her teeth into a peach as she watched Pierre placing the bacon under the grill. Reaching across, she plugged in the food mixer and whisked up eggs for scrambling.

'You're more domesticated than I thought,' Pierre said, as he poured the eggs she'd prepared into his hot pan. 'It's really surprised me, the number of skills you've acquired. When I first knew you I never imagined we'd be working together as doctors and enjoying a fantastic relationship at the same time.'

She felt her pulse quicken. Come on, Pierre, make some sort of commitment to the idea that this fantastic relationship is going to be permanent! She rearranged the cutlery she'd laid on the table while she waited, but Pierre seemed to be giving all his concentration to the eggs.

She sat down at the table and poured out two cups of coffee. 'It would be nice if this could go on and on,' she said softly.

'But it will!' Pierre said, placing a huge serving plate in front of his place at the kitchen table. 'The world's such a small place. You'll keep popping back from Hong Kong every now and again. Now that we've found each other again I don't intend to lose touch with you.'

She swallowed hard as she heard him making the point that their relationship was going to be one of convenience. He loved her but he wasn't prepared to change anything. At least that was how it sounded to her.

'More mushrooms?' he asked as he spooned some onto her plate.

'No, that's enough, thanks.' She took the plate from his hands. He was smiling at her with that heart-rendingly tender gaze that always threw her. She could feel herself melting again inside. It was impossible to harbour hard thoughts about Pierre for very long.

The shrilling of the phone broke through the peace of their breakfast. Pierre came back from the phone with a worried expression.

'Obstetrics Sister is worried about Beatrice. Her blood pressure is up again today and she's had a headache for a couple of hours.' He put a final morsel of bacon in his mouth, and while he chewed his face was a study in concentration. 'I'll schedule her Caesarean for later in the morning. I'd planned to do it in a couple of days, but we'd better bring it forward. Will you assist, Caroline?'

'Of course.'

'I'll contact Jean to set up the anaesthesia. Beatrice has known for some time that she would have to have a Caesarean and she said she definitely wants a general anaesthetic.'

'I know, she told me she wants to wake up with the twins neatly packaged in their cots,' Caroline said with a wry smile.

Pierre lifted his stethoscope from the small table by the door. 'It's much the safest way for someone with a medical history like Beatrice's. I wouldn't like to attempt a natural birth with her, especially with twins. The miscarriage she suffered last time was traumatic enough—for everyone involved.'

He shrugged into his jacket. 'Look, do you want to finish your coffee and come over later? There's no need for—'

'I'm coming now, but what about all this?' She gestured towards the debris of their breakfast.

'I can do it later. It's no problem.' He turned at the door and looked down at her, his eyes tender. 'Before we have to go all professional again, will you come out for supper with me this evening?'

The heavy oak door swung to behind them. Caroline fell into step beside Pierre.

'Two invitations in one day!' she joked, desperately trying to keep the atmosphere light. 'Breakfast and supper. I don't know if I can handle all this social life.'

'It's not social life—it's you and I making the most of the little time left to us,' he said, his voice husky and sounding so very sincere. 'After all, you'll soon be leaving here and—'

'When does Giselle come back from maternity leave?'

'The last week in October so that you can have a week together, handing over the reins and explaining what's happening in the Clinique before you go back to Hong Kong.'

'I…' she began, as mad desperation threatened to overwhelm her.

He pushed open the main door of the clinique and they crossed the reception area together.

Bending down, he looked at her quizzically. 'Sorry, you were about to say…?'

'Oh, it was nothing. Let's go up to Obstetrics.'

Beatrice was relieved when they walked in. Pierre had sent a message to Jean who was already there, preparing their patient for her Caesarean section. He removed his stethoscope, after checking her lungs, and looked up at Pierre.

'Beatrice is fit and healthy in the breathing department,' the young doctor said quietly, 'but I think we should get a move on. The headaches are getting worse and there was a touch of albumin in her urine this morning.'

Caroline frowned as she listened to the discussion of their patient. 'The presence of the albumin protein in the urine is worrying,' she said.

Both men nodded agreement. This was one of the cardinal signs that the patient might be going into the state of pre-eclampsia, which was only one step away from the life-threatening condition of eclampsia.

'The theatre's all set up, Pierre,' Jean said.

Caroline had moved to their patient's bedside. Taking hold of Beatrice's hand, she tried to reassure her that she wasn't going to suffer.

'I'm just going to give you a tiny injection in your arm, which will make you feel drowsy and a little bit thirsty. But by the time you've decided you really need a drink, we'll have given you another injection to send you completely to sleep.'

'Tell me I won't know anything until I wake up with two lovely babies beside me,' Beatrice said anxiously. 'A boy and a girl—that's what you told me when I had my last scan, wasn't it?'

Caroline smiled. 'A ready-made family.'

'Great! Because I don't mean to go through all this again, I can tell you. Michel can have the next one himself if he needs more than two. Can you give me something for this headache, Doctor?'

'I already have,' Caroline said as she withdrew the needle of the syringe from Beatrice's arm.

Minutes later they were all in Theatre.

'Everything OK your end?' Pierre asked Jean.

Dr Cadet nodded as he adjusted one of the cylinders at the head of the operating table.

Pierre looked at Caroline across the prone figure of their patient. His eyes above the mask had a confident glint as he requested a scalpel so that he could make the first incision.

She handed him the sterile instrument with her gloved hand and watched as he made a neat incision across the abdomen, before peeling back the layers of tissue to make a further incision in the lower segment of the womb.

Caroline breathed a sigh of relief as he extracted the tiny curled-up babies, who began to cry almost immediately. Theatre Sister and one of the nurses took charge of the precious bundles as Caroline and Pierre sewed back the abdominal layers.

'It's OK, Caroline,' Pierre said, as he commenced sewing the skin. 'You can go and drool over the babies if you want to.'

She smiled as she stepped down from the box which was always placed beside the table when she was assisting. She'd long since stopped being embarassed by the fact that she couldn't reach the patients if she stood on the floor. Even when Pierre had teased her at the beginning of her work at the Clinique, she hadn't minded.

Or had she grown a second skin perhaps? she wondered as she made her way to the other side of the theatre.

'Oh, they're adorable!' she said, as she took the little boy from Sister. 'And so different. This one's definitely got a thinner, more pointed face and his hair is darker than his sister's. Beatrice is going to be so thrilled with them.'

Later that afternoon, as she helped Beatrice into her own clean nightdress, she had to answer a barrage of questions about what it would be like, coping with the two delightful babies who were going to change Beatrice's life for ever.

'Don't worry about it now, Beatrice,' Caroline said gently, pulling the nightdress over her patient's head. 'You're understandably tired after your Caesarean, so you've got to rest here for a few days. By the time you're ready to go home you'll be feeling much stronger.'

'My mum's promised to help and Michel's going to take

a couple of weeks' holiday so I suppose I'll get through. And they're so beautiful, aren't they?'

Caroline leaned down to touch one of the downy heads in the two cots beside Beatrice's bed. 'They're perfect! You did an excellent job, Beatrice.'

Beatrice gave a wan smile. 'Do you really think so, Doctor? It was a bit of a strain—toeing the line like that, I mean—but it was worth it.'

Caroline patted her patient's hand. 'Of course it was.'

Later, as she discussed their patient with Pierre, she asked him if he had any doubts about Beatrice's capabilities. 'You don't think she'll revert to her previous lifestyle now she's got her babies, do you?' Caroline asked him as she looked across the table in the cosy restaurant near the main square in Montreuil.

For a moment he looked worried but the lines of anxiety soon cleared as he explained his theory concerning Beatrice.

'I think Beatrice is the sort of person who needs to have a prolonged adolescence before she settles down. Now she's got this well-balanced husband, I don't see any reason why she shouldn't be an excellent mother.'

'That's an interesting idea—a prolonged adolescence,' Caroline said, as she picked up the menu that the waiter had left on their table. 'I think there are a lot of people like that.'

She looked up at the waiter, who was hovering beside her chair. 'I'd like the king prawns, followed by the lamb, please.' She glanced across at Pierre as he ordered salmon fillet and guinea-fowl. As soon as the waiter had departed he leaned across and took hold of her hand.

'You seemed to be making a point just now—about people having a prolonged adolescence,' he said quietly.

She looked down at his fingers curled around her own and gave a sigh. 'If the cap fits…'

'Oh, come on!' He squeezed her fingers, before leaning back in his chair and giving a dismissive, light-hearted laugh. 'Nobody could ever accuse me of being adolescent, could they?'

'Only in so far as you're enjoying life on your own without any of the responsibilities of a man of your age,' she said carefully.

'I've got a *clinique* to run! And what about you? You've chosen to travel the world, living like a teenager wherever—'

'Perhaps we're both suffering from arrested development,' she put in quickly. 'But people can change and…'

She stopped talking as the waiter arrived with her prawns. Moving to one side to allow the plate to be put on the table, her eyes were drawn to a couple who'd just arrived and were being ushered over to a table by the wall. Pierre, she saw, had noticed them too.

'Isn't that Monique?' Caroline asked as soon as the waiter had gone.

Pierre nodded. 'I wonder who she's with?'

'Probably her boyfriend.'

Pierre was dissecting his salmon with the precision of a surgeon performing a delicate operation. 'She hasn't got a boyfriend,' he said, without looking up. 'And the chap she's with must be years younger than she is.'

'How do you know she hasn't got a boyfriend?' Caroline asked innocently as she popped one of the succulent prawns into her mouth, savouring the subtle hint of garlic in the sauce.

'Because she told me she preferred to keep out of relationships that would cramp her style. No, Monique is only interested in herself. She's incapable of sharing her life with anyone.'

'Then the two of you were well suited to each other,' she said quickly, her heart beginning to beat madly as she realised she was risking alienation from Pierre again.

'What do you mean by that?' he asked slowly, putting down his fork on the side of his plate and rinsing his fingers in the lemon-scented finger bowl.

'Well, you both prefer to be independent,' she said.

'It takes one to know one,' he replied, his eyes intently watching her reaction.

She put down her fork and met his gaze. 'I've come to the conclusion that independence is no good without love,' she said slowly. 'And love needs commitment.'

'What are you trying to say?'

As she took a deep breath she heard the shrilling of the mobile phone in her bag. It was her turn on call tonight, and she was instantly on the alert.

'Don't worry, I'll go back to the Clinique with you if there's an emergency,' Pierre said as she put the receiver to her ear.

'David! Sorry, what was that? It's a bad line, I can't...' She looked across at Pierre who was watching her quizzically. 'It's my boss from Hong Kong.'

Pierre frowned. 'Is there a problem?'

The crackling on the line stopped and she clearly heard David talking about sending references for her new job.

'I can't talk now,' she said quickly. 'I'll phone you later.'

'I've got to go to Singapore for a conference and I won't be available for a couple of weeks so...'

'No hurry,' she said. 'I'll call you when you get back. Goodbye, David.'

Pierre was still watching her intently. 'Why couldn't you

talk now?' he asked. 'Is there something you don't want me to hear?'

Suddenly, all the trouble of beating about the bush didn't seem worth it. She would burn her boats and take the consequences! It seemed as if all the paths leading up to her life with Pierre were converging, and either they would stay on the same road together or they would go their separate ways.

She glanced across at Monique who was happily chatting to her young boyfriend. Ever since Giselle had told her about him she'd been convinced that Monique would welcome the chance to get her hands on some cash from the sale of her half of the château.

'I'll discuss it with you when we go back to the château, Pierre,' she said, evenly.

'But—'

'No, I can't have you blowing your top in front of the entire restaurant.'

'That bad, is it?'

'It could be,' she replied, knowing that she had the power to create an explosion!

## CHAPTER ELEVEN

'Do you think you could take me out of my suspense now?' Pierre asked.

Caroline settled herself comfortably at the other side of the sofa, having insisted that she didn't want him to sit too close until she'd finished her explanation. He poured himself another glass of wine, having downed the first one in seconds.

He smiled across the divide of cushions between them. 'You're making me nervous.'

'That makes two of us. This could be the end of our relationship.' She took a deep breath to steady her nerves. 'I've burned my boats as far as Hong Kong is concerned. I'm not going back. Now, I know how much you value your independence. I felt the same way until…until I came back here and—'

He reached across and pulled her, protesting, into his arms. 'Are you trying to tell me that you've changed?' he asked, his voice husky with emotion.

'Yes, but I know how you feel about—'

'No, you don't know how I feel. Ever since you came back I've wanted to ask you to stay on but I was sure you wouldn't agree. You'd told me all about how you'd been schooled by your mother and your grandmother to keep your independence. And after jet-setting around the world, living in exotic places, I thought you wouldn't want to be tied down to—'

'Tied down to this château!' Her voice rose as she

started to laugh with the sheer relief she was feeling at Pierre's reaction

'I'd be over the moon to be tied to this château for the rest of my life. Don't worry, I'm not going to offer to buy into this place because I know you'd turn me down, but what's wrong with taking up your dad's offer? You saw Monique and her boyfriend tonight. Giselle told me Monique needs the money to keep him in the style he's becoming accustomed to so why don't you—?'

'I'm going to have to swallow my pride if I ask Dad to—'

'It's your inheritance, Pierre!' She stirred in his arms so that she could look up at him. His face was animated but guarded.

'I know. I was very annoyed when my father refused to sanction the money when I first needed it, but—'

'But he didn't know you were going to make such a success of the Clinique. And you were going to marry Monique and he didn't approve of her, did he?'

'He certainly didn't.' He paused as his arms tightened around her. 'But he definitely approves of the girl I'd like to marry now, if she'll have me—if she's really sure she wants to stay here.'

She felt a surge of sensual emotion as she snuggled closer in his arms. 'Who's this mythical girl you're talking about? She sounds like a paragon of—'

'She's a stubborn, self-willed, impossible, wonderful woman I've known all my life who never ceases to amaze me. Caroline, darling, please, say yes. Will you marry me?'

Hours later, she couldn't remember what she'd said exactly. Her reply had been some incoherent babble which Pierre had silenced halfway through with a kiss that had reduced her to such depths of longing that he'd picked her up in his arms and carried her up to his room.

As they lay together now, with the moonlight streaming in through the open window, she stirred in his arms, revelling in the strong muscular feel of his limbs and the musky, male scent of him.

'Are you sure you've got a permanent post for me here at the Clinique?'

'Ah, it's practicalities now, is it?' he said, stroking her damp hair with one hand while the other caressed her shoulder. 'Actually, I've been meaning to take on another permanent doctor for some time now. And you and Giselle work extremely well together. We'll have to arrange that you both get pregnant at different times, though.'

She traced a finger over the curves of his boyish grin. 'How do you feel about children?'

'I think they're fairly necessary to the continuation of the species, and—'

'Pierre, be serious for a moment. This is one of the subjects that we should agree on.'

'If they're all as wonderful as their mother I'd like about six.'

'Six!'

'Well, five, then.'

'Four! And that's my last offer!'

He clasped her hand. 'Going, going, gone! Sold to the lady with the sexiest birthday suit in this bed…'

## EPILOGUE

CAROLINE came out of the bathroom, her face wreathed in smiles. Her bare feet seemed to hug the long pile of the bedroom carpet as she skipped back into bed. How should she break the wonderful news?

She ran her fingers down Pierre's bare arm, lingering over the part of his wrist that remained white because of his watch strap. It was still early in May but the sun had been warm in the bluebell woods yesterday, and his tan was already showing. She sighed. Was it possible that it was only a year since she'd arrived here from her other life in Hong Kong?

'You know the farmhouse is up for sale?' she said carefully.

Pierre put his breakfast coffee-cup down on the bedside table on which was scattered the various sections of the Saturday edition of *Le Figaro* which he'd been down to the village to collect. His expression was quizzical as he turned to look at her.

'I had heard it was going to change hands, yes. Apparently, the farmer and his wife are retiring to a small cottage on the coast and the sons are going to work in the new computer business in Montreuil.'

'They've already sold most of the land to one of the other farmers so it's just the farmhouse, the garden and a couple of fields,' she said in a light tone, as she hugged the secret close to her heart.

He reached across and drew her against him. 'Darling, why all this sudden interest in the farmhouse?'

181

She took a deep breath. 'Because I think we should buy it. This bedroom is too small for a bed and a cot and—'

He let out a whoop of pure joy and clasped her tighter in his arms. 'Is that why you looked so happy when you came out of the bathroom? You've done a test… You got a positive result… Darling, that's wonderful!'

His tender kiss deepened. She savoured the blissful moment, one of many they'd shared together since she'd moved into this little love nest.

They'd been married a few days before Christmas. A sprinkling of snow had covered the roof of the village church, making it look like a picture postcard setting as she'd walked up the path in her long white velvet gown, she remembered. Her stepsisters, Suzanne and Charlotte, had come over from Hong Kong for the wedding, and—surprise of surprises—they'd managed to contact her father and he'd made a flying visit to give her away.

He hadn't changed! He'd looked slightly older than she remembered, but he was still unrepentant about the way he'd treated the women in his life. He'd seemed to expect her to welcome him with open arms. Whilst she'd found it difficult to do that, she'd deliberately subdued her feelings of resentment for the occasion. Weddings and Christmas were times for forgiveness.

Many former patients had turned up for the occasion. Particularly welcome had been Gregoire and Katie who'd tied their own knot in the New Year. Katie's mother had told Caroline that she entirely approved of her daughter marrying Gregoire. They both knew the score as far as their health was concerned and it seemed pointless to deny the true happiness that they shared.

Thinking back to her wedding day now, Caroline reflected that her father had appeared to be financially stable and she hadn't asked any questions about his current wife.

Perhaps he'd finally found what he'd been looking for in life.

She certainly had! She looked up at Pierre, raising one of her fingers to trace his beloved features. She understood every nuance of his character now. She knew that he still held a strong streak of independence in his character. But it didn't impinge on their relationship. They were both pretty tough characters and if they had a difference of opinion over something it didn't change their rock-solid love for each other.

'So, about this farmhouse,' Pierre said with a wry smile. 'You've given the matter some thought, I take it.'

She laughed. Now came the true confessions! 'Actually, your mother and I…'

'Ah, so Maman has been influencing you, has she?'

'Only in so far as Sylvie and I talked about how you and I would cope with a family in these small rooms, and decided…' She paused as she watched him rolling his eyes up at the ceiling.

He grinned. 'Go on, tell me what you and Maman decided.'

'Well, you know they're on the point of selling their Paris apartment now that your mother has decided to retire. They asked me to check out that cottage that was for sale in the village. I told them I thought it was too small. So when I heard about the farmhouse I discussed it with Sylvie. She said it would be perfect if she and Christophe could have the farm cottage and we could have the farmhouse. That way she'd be able to help with the grandchildren when I was on duty and Christophe would be able to help you in the Clinique when you needed him.'

Pierre threw back his head and laughed. 'Caroline, you never cease to amaze me! You'd got this all sewn up before you even knew whether you were pregnant or not.'

'Well, we had been practising fairly hard, hadn't we? I thought there was a pretty good chance that one of those millions of little sperm had swum in the right direction.'

He sighed. 'I've enjoyed practising. You're not going to be one of those women who go off sex when they're pregnant, are you?'

She snuggled closer, running her hands over his bare chest. 'I don't know. We'd better do some research and find out, Doctor. From the way I'm feeling at the moment, I would say that pregnancy is having a very peculiar effect on me…'

# MILLS & BOON®

## *Makes*
## *any time*
## *special*

### *Enjoy a romantic novel from*
### *Mills & Boon*®

*Presents...*™     *Enchanted*™     TEMPTATION.

*Historical Romance*™     ⁄MEDICAL
                          ROMANCE®

MILLS & BOON®

# ⟋ℓ MEDICAL ROMANCE™

### THE COURAGE TO SAY YES by Lilian Darcy
*Southshore #2 of 4*

Paediatric surgeon Angus Ferguson had seen Caitlin Gray's fiancé, Scott, with another woman. Could he persuade her to see through Scott and look favourably on himself?

### DOCTORS IN CONFLICT by Drusilla Douglas

The attraction between Catriona MacFarlane, the new Medical Registrar, and Michael Preston, orthopaedic surgeon, was *definitely* mutual, but when they both had such set ideas, how would they learn to compromise?

### THE PERFECT TREATMENT by Rebecca Lang

Dr Abby Gibson was thrilled to discover she would be working with highly esteemed Dr Blake Contini. Although it was obvious from his warm smiling manner that Blake liked her, *something* was stopping him offering more than friendship...

### PERFECT TIMING by Alison Roberts
*The dawn of a new age...*

Surgeon Jack Armstrong and nurse Amanda Morrison clashed horribly. It was their mutual delight in an elderly patient who would be one hundred years old on the first day of the new Millennium that brought them closer...

## Available from 3rd December 1999

**MILLENNIUM**

**Celebrate the Millennium with your favourite romance authors. With so many to choose from, there's a Millennium story for everyone!**

*Presents...™*

**Morgan's Child**
**Anne Mather**
On sale 3rd December 1999

*Enchanted™*

**Bride 2000**
**Trisha David**
On sale 3rd December 1999

**TEMPTATION®**

**Once a Hero**
**Kate Hoffmann**
On sale 3rd December 1999

**Always a Hero**
**Kate Hoffmann**
On sale 7th January 2000

**⌁MEDICAL**
**ROMANCE™**

**Perfect Timing**
**Alison Roberts**
On sale 3rd December 1999

MILLS & BOON®

*Makes any time special™*

# MILLS & BOON®

# MISTLETOE *Magic*

Three favourite Enchanted™ authors
bring you romance at Christmas.

Three stories in one volume:

### *A Christmas Romance*
### BETTY NEELS

### *Outback Christmas*
### MARGARET WAY

### *Sarah's First Christmas*
### REBECCA WINTERS

*Published 19th November 1999*

*Available at most branches of WH Smith, Tesco,
Martins, Borders, Easons, Volume One/James Thin
and most good paperback bookshops*

## 2 Books
### and a surprise gift!

We would like to take this opportunity to thank you for reading this Mills & Boon® book by offering you the chance to take TWO more specially selected titles from the Medical Romance™ series absolutely FREE! We're also making this offer to introduce you to the benefits of the Reader Service™—

- ★ FREE home delivery
- ★ FREE gifts and competitions
- ★ FREE monthly Newsletter
- ★ Books available before they're in the shops
- ★ Exclusive Reader Service discounts

Accepting these FREE books and gift places you under no obligation to buy; you may cancel at any time, even after receiving your free shipment. Simply complete your details below and return the entire page to the address below. *You don't even need a stamp!*

**YES!** Please send me 2 free Medical Romance books and a surprise gift. I understand that unless you hear from me, I will receive 4 superb new titles every month for just £2.40 each, postage and packing free. I am under no obligation to purchase any books and may cancel my subscription at any time. The free books and gift will be mine to keep in any case.

M9EB

Ms/Mrs/Miss/Mr .................................................Initials.............................
BLOCK CAPITALS PLEASE

Surname........................................................................................

Address........................................................................................

........................................................................................

........................................................Postcode ........................

**Send this whole page to:**
**UK: The Reader Service, FREEPOST CN81, Croydon, CR9 3WZ**
**EIRE: The Reader Service, PO Box 4546, Kilcock, County Kildare (stamp required)**

Offer not valid to current Reader Service subscribers to this series. We reserve the right to refuse an application and applicants must be aged 18 years or over. Only one application per household. Terms and prices subject to change without notice. Offer expires 31st May 2000. As a result of this application, you may receive further offers from Harlequin Mills & Boon Limited and other carefully selected companies. If you would prefer not to share in this opportunity please write to The Data Manager at the address above.

Mills & Boon is a registered trademark owned by Harlequin Mills & Boon Limited.
Medical Romance is being used as a trademark.

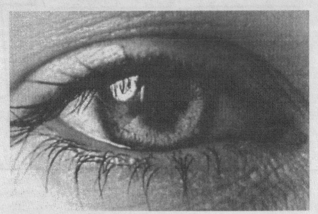

# SWEET REVENGE

# NORA ROBERTS

Adrianne led a remarkable double life.
Daughter of a Hollywood beauty and an
Arab playboy, the paparazzi knew her as a
frivolous socialite darting from exclusive
party to glittering charity ball. But no one
knew her as The Shadow, a jewel thief with
a secret ambition to carry out the ultimate
robbery—a plan to even the score.

The Shadow was intent on justice.

**Published 22nd October**